BOCA LUPO

PANOS KAZOLIS
BOCA LUPO

TRANSLATER:
STAVROULA ZARRA
TO MY FRIEND NESTOR

CHAPTER 1

The young man tactfully wiped his sweaty palms on his back pockets, took a deep breath to control his heartbeat, and cleared his throat for the second time, trying to grab the attention of the bloated man behind the counter. The guy dropped his pen on the papers in front of him and sluggishly raised his head.

"What is it?"

The kid gulped. "So sorry to bother you, but I've been waiting for five minutes, and…"

"What?"

"Are you Mr. Tzanis?"

The attendant's gaze became invigorated for about three seconds, just until a curvaceous woman with yellow tights crossed the street then disappeared from his field of vision. He sighed and maintained his gaze out the windows, worried about missing the next spectacle. "So what do you want?"

The young man, who was very uncomfortable and not used to being bullied, cowered for a second but plucked up his courage and resolved to try again. "Soulis has sent me."

The guy turned around and looked straight at him for the first time. "Soulis, the coffee shop owner?"

"Yes, that's him."

"Why haven't you said so?"

"I have, but you're not listening!" The young man started to get upset because he had been trying for months to find a way out of the merchant trade, so it irritated him even more when the clerk started laughing at him.

"Relax; don't get defensive. You're right, but have you seen the girls passing by?" He whistled, but the kid kept his gaze on Tzanis, waiting.

Tzanis scratched his unshaven mug, observed for a moment the young man who was staring at him in silence, then smiled warmly and leaned forward. "Soulis rang me yesterday on your behalf. Isn't your name Panagiotakis?"

The young man nodded, and Tzanis, the shipping agent, widened his smile. "You see, I remember. And you want to go to sea, don't you?"

"Yes." The heartbeat of hope engulfed the youngster once more, who attempted to control his excitement by lighting up a cigarette.

"Let's pretend I've got something for you. Are you sure you can make it? It's a tough game."

'Yes...'

'And what kind of vessel would you like to go on board, mate?'

The heartbeat of hope engulfed the youngster once more, who attempted to control his excitement by lighting up a cigarette.

'What do you mean what kind of vessel?'

'What kind of ship, my boy? A cargo ship?'

Charged with great intensity, the youngster shook his head from side to side, staring straight at Tzanis. 'No'.

The agent's grin became playful.

'Then maybe a tanker, an ore-carrier, or a ferry?'

'No, way. I can find these anywhere.'

'What, then?'

'A potato freighter, mate. I'm looking for a potato freighter...'

Tzanis chuckled and leaned back into his armchair. 'That's it. That's what Soulis' said, but I wanted to hear it from you.'

'Well then, now you've heard.'

'Take it easy, lad. Let's pretend I've got something for you. Are you sure you can make it? It's a tough game.'

The youngster stooped over him very eagerly. "Don't you worry about that. Tough is what I'm after, too, as long as it's reflected in the dough. Is there a place?"

Tzanis stood up from his armchair, scratching his mug again. "Listen. There is a position, but even Soulis, who recommended you, doesn't know much about you. Between us, he doesn't know anything. If I do send you and you're not right, I'll lose face with people I'd rather not. How can I be sure you'll make it? Do you get me?"

With his heart beating like the tambourine, the young man lowered himself a little more toward him and tried his best to make his voice more convincing. "As far as I know, Mr. Tzanis, you've been around the block for a while, and I don't think you would have wasted your time with me if you felt I couldn't hack it. Am I right?" His muscular body was tense with anxiety, and he spent the next few seconds observing Tzanis, who was looking at him, lost in thought.

The attendant stopped scratching and stretched out his hand with a smile. "All right, dude. I'm sold. Let's shake on it. Welcome to the wild side."

"I don't understand. I mean...how?"

"Can you fly to Dubrovnik, tomorrow?"

The young man grinned from ear to ear. "I can fly right now."

"Have you got a passport on you?"

"I've also got my seaman's book."

"Leave that; you won't be needing it." He opened the drawer, threw the passport in, and pulled a bankroll out. "That's for painting the town red tonight, but be here at midday tomorrow to get to the airport on time."

It was nearly dusk as the dazed youngster stepped out the door and into the humidity that blanketed the Greek Miaouli Coast. He hovered by a corner, sucking in the air of the port, overwhelmed by the unique taste of triumph. Feeling like he was gliding on air, he wandered for a while before he disappeared into the dump that had been harboring his dreams every night for the past few months.

The artificial redhead behind the bar was surprised. "Are you smiling, Panos, or do I need an eye doctor?"

"Hello, Lena. How are you getting on, doll?"

"Compliments, too, Panos? Smiles and compliments? You're spoiling me."

"Don't say another word, my little Lena, and prepare a double for me, treat the lads, and pour whatever you fancy for yourself."

The redhead was in shock. "What is it, love? Have you won the lottery?"

"You could say that, my little Lena. You could say that…"

For young Panagiotis, this was the lottery, and he spent two whole years trying to win it, but something always went wrong and messed things up at the last minute. But with every obstacle, he became more stubborn and refused to give up. He searched, enquired, bummed around, greased the palms of many people, wasted his money—and mostly his time—when, out of nowhere, Soulis, the coffee shop owner, came through for him, making him the winner of his wager with the boatswain.

The boatswain was certain. "It's impossible, you guys. These are closed business circles. They won't let just any-one in."

Young Panagiotis jumped in like a cockerel. "If it's true, I bet you boss I can get in!"

That was the first time ever that the bosun had ever mentioned it, and since he seemed in a particularly good mood that evening, they didn't quite believe him.

"That's just big talk, boss. What the hell…We would've heard. It's just a lie."

The boatswain looked at the sea. It'd been really calm for the past three days and nights, since they'd left Lisbon, which was all the more convenient for them, as they could enjoy their drinks on deck number three, the most spacious one. They were having a relatively pleasant time, talking about their dreams and their chicks. The boatswain would repeat stories he'd told them before about the time-worn ship Hope as it sailed toward New York.

"It's not a lie, you idiots. It's the truth. A cousin of mine used to work there. I would have joined as well if it weren't for the family."

"What does family have to do with this, boss?"

"When you have children, you don't play tough games. You tone down your manliness and play the fool to bring your kids up. That's what!"

"Is it hard, boss?"

"My cousin lasted six months by the skin of his teeth!"

Flushed from curiosity and whiskey, Lalakis, the chubby youth from Hydra, was hanging on his every word. "How about the cargo? All of it illegal? A shipful?"

"Yeah, man. I'm talking about many shipfuls. There must be over twenty going about this business in the Mediterranean."

"And the dosh, boss? Are they paying well?"

The bosun made a weighing gesture with his hands. "Tons of money!"

The rough sailor from Volos, Mitsos, couldn't take it any longer. "Why shouldn't we get aboard as well, boss? Why the hell are we drowning in this wreck for nothing?"

"They rarely need new people, Mitso. They are just a few, and if they happen to need anyone, they stick to their own."

"Then there's no way we can get in?"

The bosun shook his head no, so, Panagiotakis, the butting-in idiot, placed the wager.

CHAPTER 2

The pilot gained the required height, turned off the seatbelt and smoking signs, and the youngster waived his hand at the air hostess to come over to him.

"Coffee, please, and a whiskey."

He emptied the miniature bottle into his coffee, took a sip, and opened the newspaper he'd picked up on his way in. He tried to relax by reading, but his hands were shaking, the letters started dancing, and, when he saw his smudged palms, he was sick of it and started looking for somewhere to shove it in.

The adjacent bearded guy, with a ridiculous tie, pre-empted him, smiling. "May I?"

With a sadistic desire for someone else to get his hands filthy, he returned the smile to the bearded guy and got rid of the paper. He leaned back again, gazed at Attica's peninsula for a while as it receded from view, slowly being dwarfed by the Aegean Sea, and his mind wandered off to Lenio, the redhead, who lied beside him the night before, stark naked and sweaty, controlling her panting, asked him once more in a whisper, "Will you remember me?"

He got up from the bed with difficulty and approached the mirror, fanning his neck with his palm.

Lenio did her best all morning to charge his batteries with memories he could take with him from Greece. He barely managed to get an hour of sleep, so by midday, on his way to his rendezvous with Tzanis, his knees were giving way and his eyes were reminiscent of a vampire.

Tzanis cracked up. "What happened to you, Panagiotakis? Did you spend the night in jail?"

"Just about..."

"I see, but you have to keep your strength, 'cuz you'll need it. And, by the way, make sure you hide the hickey on your neck."

"Is it very noticeable?"

"Not if you're not looking...Leave that for now, and listen to what I have to tell you..."

On their way to the airport, Tzanis briefed the young man about where he's going and what to expect. "As you can probably understand, what counts most is honor and heart. If you're real, you're gonna have a good time and rake it in. If not, you'll come back broke and disgraced."

The young man's red eyes resembled burning coal. "I've told you before; you don't have to worry. Who did you say will be expecting me?"

"His name's Charis. Nice guy."

CHAPTER 3

The captain switched on his lights again, recited the obligatory poem about weathers and ground temperatures as the bearded guy turned to Panos. "That was a good landing. Here's your newspaper."

The kid pulled his hands back. "All yours."

It'd been half an hour since he'd gone through passport control, and he still hadn't spotted anyone waiting for him. He looked over, one by one, everyone who was wandering around the waiting area. Looking intently at some who seemed fitting, a couple of them had misunderstood him, and he started to worry he was going to cause a problem with his strange behavior. Soon the crowd thinned out, and the employees stared at him suspiciously. The young man collected his suitcase and went out onto the street. He looked bewilderedly up and down, then made for his left, changed his mind, turned right, took a few steps, thought better of it, and finally returned to sit on a short stone wall next to the entrance.

Half an hour later, still on the wall, he went through his pockets for the third time to find any forgotten money, cursing himself out loud for his stupid idea to give away to Lenio the leftover bills from the previous night's binging. He was huffing and puffing, not knowing what to do, when a beaten-up Zastava drove up noisily next the entrance and stopped.

The kid dug into his brain to find the English required to ask where the port was, but when he saw the driver of the car, changed his mind and sat back down. Long haired, unwashed, and unshaven for many days, a tall guy with dirty jeans banged on the Zastava's door, which jangled all its parts, then he rushed, frenzied, back into the waiting room. Panos looked at the road again, figuring that since ports are always low, it was wise to start going downhill, which should get him at least a bit closer to where he needed to be. The tall grimy guy, who dashed back out, barely had time to stop before bumping into him. "Sorry!"

"Go to hell, wanker! You almost killed me!"

"Are you Greek, mate? You're not Panagiotakis, by any chance?"

Panagiotakis, who was a bit lost, looked him up and down.

"Yes, that's me. Don't tell me you're Charis!"

Charis followed the kid's stare and burst out laughing.

"I guess I didn't catch your eye?"

"No, it's alright. Sorry I cussed at you; I took you for a Yugoslavian."

"Don't worry about it, no big deal. I'm such a mess, not even my mother would want to be near me. Have you got anything else with you?"

"Just this suitcase."

"Cool; Throw it in, and let's go. I'll fill you in on the way."

The jalopy's engine started after the fourth attempt, and it set off rattling toward the opposite direction than the one he had selected earlier. "Aren't you worried it's going to break down?"

"I am, but we have to make do; we can't get any better. Only two or three are good, and whoever gets here first rents them. There are no luxuries in this place."

They drove through picturesque Dubrovnik, but Charis didn't slow down at all, and Panos found it strange. "Aren't we going to the port?"

"Yes, but not this one. We're on our way to Plotche, Yogoslavia."

"What's that? What' d you call it?"

"Plotche? It's just a seaport, about an hour's drive away, but tell me more about you. Where are you from, Panagiotakis?"

Panos answered this and many more questions about his past, his schooling, and his experience at sea, but when Charis entered private territory, Panos got annoyed.

"Hang on, Charis. Why do you flippin' care if I'm married or not? Are you a matchmaker or something?"

A kind-hearted bloke, Charis burst out laughing so hard, he almost lost control of the vehicle.

"No, definitely not a matchmaker, Panagiotakis. I'm the captain."

Panos bit his lips. "The captain? I've screwed up again. I thought you were an oiler..."

"Yeah, you're not wrong there."

"Sorry, Captain Charis, but how..."

Charis completed the question himself, since the youngster wouldn't dare, afraid of crossing the line. "How come a mighty captain is running around like a scruff?"

The youth decided not to speak, and Charis went on. "For starters, no more Captain shit. You just call me Charis, like everyone else, and, to brief you, there are seven of us all in all on board, and formalities among us are a stupid luxury. We're not the merchant navy here. That is to say, we're still merchants, but without customs procedures, as it were. Are you following me?"

"More than enough. Go on..."

The captain reached behind his car seat, fumbling and feeling among the greasy parts on the floor, and pulled out a bottle of whiskey. He took a slug and passed it on to the kid. "Well, Panagiotakis, we're seven souls, you know, risking with the contraband to make a packet. That's our goal. Are you following me?"

The young man nodded.

"As the captain, so to speak, I'm in charge, though everyone can voice their opinion and we make the decisions together when it concerns something serious. Of course, we all carry our personal baggage, but in a difficult situation we come together as a family, like a fist, so to speak. Are you following me?"

This time the young man only looked at him, and Charis went on. "You'll meet the rest soon, if I manage to get there myself!"

"What do you mean?"

"We've had a problem with the electricity engine for five days now. We completely dismantled it, but no luck. Finally, the Italian guy brought us the spares today, and we tackled it. I had to pick you up, but the rest must be still trying to repair it. I hope we finish off with the engine tonight, so we can load up tomorrow."

"So, Captain Charis, how's the work done? At night, on the sly?"

"No, Panagiotakis. The cigarettes are imported legally. Are you following me? The Italians buy them from various factories in Europe and send them packaged here on transit trains—legitimately."

"Always here, in Plotche?"

"Wherever is more convenient, but always in the Adriatic. Albania or Yugoslavia."

"Why especially there?"

"Because of their regimes, as they don't give a damn where the cigarettes go next. Provided they receive their taxes and their rake-off. We, let's say, declare Lebanon as our destination, they get their bribe, and sign the sailing without questions, even waving goodbye when we put out to sea."

"They are waving you goodbye?"

"Everywhere, always and forever."

"Why, Captain Charis? Out of love?"

"We dole out a lot of money, Panagiotakis."

"I see. And the cargo? Where does it finally go?"

"We work Italy. Some others France, depending on which squadra you collaborate with."

"You mean the owners of the cargo?"

"Yes, they're something of a cooperative, let's say. They raise money, buy the cargo, and ship it to us in the Adriatic, wherever we want. Then we deliver it to Italy, wherever they want. Are you following me?"

"Yes, fine, but the unloading takes place on the sly, doesn't it?"

"That's exactly what we're getting paid for, Panagiotakis."

"And what do they do afterward?"

"They work normally, almost like every other business. They sell it on to others, put their money together, buy a new load, split the profit, and start fresh, like they say. Our job ends, though, the moment we deliver the cargo to the speedboats."

Fascinated by speedboats from an early age, Panos was intrigued. "When you say speedboats, how speedy are they?"

"As fast as arrows, Panagiotakis. They take the cargo from us mid-sea and carry it ashore. Naturally, they face the most dangers."

"Why is that?"

"We get chased sometimes, too, but they are being pursued by Gods and Demons, like they say."

"They must be getting paid loads, I guess, aren't they? How much, really?"

"The speedboat coxwains? It could be even ten times more than you are."

Panos startled like he had been stung by a wasp. "Did you just say ten times? Is it possible for me to do this job, Captain Charis?"

Charis, who had been knocking back the last sip in the bottle, almost choked from his laughter. Then he cleared his throat and became serious. "What the hell are you talking about, Panagiotakis? Believe me, I appreciate it that you don't seem to balk at difficulties, but, this business, lad, is for Premier League professionals, not just anyone. Many have tried, few have succeeded. Are you following me?"

The kid decided to go along with him. "Where exactly are we unloading?"

"I don't know yet. Franco, the Italian who brought us the spares, is going to travel with us as the cargo attendant. If we finish tomorrow, he is going to confer on the phone with his guys in Italy, they'll tell us the position they want, and off we go."

The grey afternoon fit Plotche like a glove, which, lacking the architectural magnificence of Dubrovnik, resembled its poor relative. Panos gazed briefly at the dark multi-storey cages and screwed up his face. "It's a disgusting-looking city."

Charis agreed. "Yeah, and jinxed, too. As soon as we arrived, our ship got damaged. Next trip, we're going elsewhere."

There was almost no traffic on the roads, yet Charis had been driving carefully, at a low speed up to the center of the city, crossing Tito's six-floor high, sullen face, before stepping on the accelerator again toward the port. Moaning, groaning, and gambolling like a goat on cobblestone, the small Zastava stopped at the gate of the port in one piece, earning Panos's admiration. "There's still life in the old dog, after all! Why have you stopped? Aren't we going in?"

"There's no reason. They have probably finished and left."

"How can you tell from here?"

"The other cars are missing from the front of the ship. This means they've gone."

"What ship? Is that it?"

Just then he noticed the half-erased letters on the bow.

"Brother, it's a wreck."

Empty of cargo, the Salonica was gliding high on the water, with its rust looking like a military camouflage uniform. Pitch-dark, it took the shape of a cast-off, decommissioned corpse. Winking cheekily, Charis smiled.

"It's not a wreck, Panagiotakis. That's the fib, so that it won't grab attention. Parading is not in our interest. Are you following me?" Panos had stopped answering the stupid question ages ago.

"Are we going to wait for them to come back here?"

"We're not waiting for anyone. This is the ship; you've seen it, and tomorrow you'll see it even better. Let's go to the hotel now to take a shower and dress up, become human again. I stink like a cesspit."

Panos looked at him, shocked.

"Did you say hotel? Don't we sleep on board?"

A cheerful bloke, Charis never missed an opportunity to laugh. "Sleep on board—while we're docked? You must be out of your mind. We never stay in unless we're travelling."

An oasis of faded luxury, the hotel, the pride of the city, felt imposing and almost deserted. Designed for grandeur, the massive chandelier in the middle of the foyer with half its bulbs burnt out dimly illuminated the gloom of vast hall, as well as the company of some elderly German tourists who were enjoying their coffee in silence, and the bald patch of the chubby, jolly bloke that walked straight to them.

"Finalmente, capitano!"

"Ciao, Franco! Come Va?"

They had a brief conversation in Italian, gesticulating, and then Charis turned to Panos. "Panagiotakis, let me introduce you to Franco, the guy I was telling you about. Franco, this is Panagiotakis."

Franco leaned forward to understand better. "Come?"

"Pa-na-gio-ta-kis."

The Italian stretched his neck even closer, but still couldn't get it. "Molto, difficile. Che cosa significa?"

Charis looked at Panos. "He is asking what Panagiotakis means."

"I don't know. Holy, all-holy, Holy Mother, that sort of thing..."

"Well done; that's it. Holy Mother; that is Mary. So... Mario!"

Panos shrugged, and Charis turned triumphantly to the Italian. "Panagiotaki significa Mario."

Relieved to have got the difficulty out of the way, the Italian held out his hand. "Piacere, Mario."

The captain had asked him to meet again in an hour, but Panos, who felt the drab room suffocating him, got ready quickly, changed clothes, and went downstairs twenty minutes early. The new group of German tourists that had joined the others already sitting in the hotel lounge hadn't altered the hotel lounge ambience in the slightest. It retained its funereal quietness, in keeping with the surroundings and the employees' faces. Panos ordered a whiskey, took it with him, and settled in a spot where he could look outside at the deserted street with the yellow lights. Dressed to impress, polished and elegant like a model, Captain Charis appeared on the staircase at nine o'clock sharp, precisely when Panos was waving at the waiter to bring him his second drink.

Charis stopped the waiter, cancelled the drink, and ordered a bottle. Then he approached Panos, who stood up.

"There's no need for a bottle, Captain Charis. I'll be fine with two more."

"Of course there is! You'll see it won't be enough to go 'round, not even to say cheers. But where are the others? Haven't they come down yet?"

"I haven't seen anyone."

"Scamps! I told them the same time. Anyway, Pan— sorry, Mario, well done, my friend, for being punctual. This is a skill, take my word for it, so be careful not to lose it. It's important. Are you following me?"

Suddenly the room was animated with the bang from a door shut with a kick and voices and the clatter of feet that followed. The Germans looked apprehensively at each other.

"Here they are, Mario: our gems."

Out of the four men coming down the stairs, three were arguing while the fourth that was following on was hopping down, pretending to be lame. When he reached them, panting, he put his leg down and stood still, waiting. The elderly Germans discovered a gratuitous spectacle to fill their dreary time, disdained the miserable street view, turned their seats around to take a closer look at the rowdy bunch, their countenance pepped up, and they remembered that they possess a language in which to communicate.

The three men kept on quarrelling, the Germans bucked up, so they too started teasing each other and laughing, while the Yugoslav employees half-awakened to serve, and the waiter hurried off to put on a cassette tape with Greek songs, just to calm things down.

"Oi, shut up for a minute and listen!" This was the third time the captain had screamed his lungs out to get noticed, and it finally worked.

"Sit down! Have you no shame! We've been ridiculed again. And we call the others barbarians!"

"We also call them corpses."

"OK, Corfiot. That's fine. We call them corpses, too, but why have you come down here hopping? Are you completely bonkers?"

The man from Corfu was taken aback. "Why not? Has anyone complained?"

"You should be locked up, but, seriously, having a crew of barmy people, is really a testament to my sanity. Maybe that's why I don't get cross enough to smash your face in! Are you following me? Anyway, let's leave this for now, this lad here is Mario, and he'll probably be working with me on the bridge. What do you say Mario? You've got enough experience; can you handle it?"

Panos was disconcerted. "I'll try..."

"I'll teach you everything you need. I believe you have it in you. Well then, let me introduce the gang one by one. This is Makis, the engineer. He's from Lefkas."

The sturdy thirty-five-year-old with a coarse but likeable countenance and as square as a piece of furniture shook Panos's hand tightly. "Makis."

"Welcome aboard, mate."

Charis pointed at the next one. "You've already met Spyros, the loopy Corfiot. His brother used to be with us as well, but he left us last week. You've replaced him."

No more than twenty-five, the Corfiot, dapper, cute, and cool, stretched his hand out, smiling. "Hello, Mario! Welcome to our crew."

"Thanks, Spyros. Why has your brother left?"

"Ah! He got tired after almost two years of nonstop work and—" He stopped abruptly and looked crossly at the man next to him. "Why are you laughing, Phaedo, you wanker. Am I lying? Hasn't he worked for two years?"

"And got tired? Yeah, man; you're lying. What was he doing to get tired? Digging?"

Spyros stared at him with utter contempt. "Do you only get tired when you dig, you moron? Aren't there any other reasons?"

"Yes, of course there are! Like changing underpants every five minutes." He was still speaking when he positioned himself in order to shield any blows from the Corfiot's reaction, who stood up, enraged. However, the captain's banging fist on the table cut them short and capsized two glasses.

"Calm down at last, you rogues!"

The Corfiot returned to his seat with slow movements, and Phaedo turned to his front again, disappointing the Germans, who were expecting the show to go on.

"As for you, Phaedo, I don't know what's bitten you lately, but, brother, you've gone too far, and if you keep this up on the voyage, I'll send you packing, to be honest with you. Are you following me?"

Phaedo locked his tiny eyes on Charis, but didn't say a word. The captain took a sip from his drink and turned to Mario. "OK, then, let's pretend you've met him as well. The other one, the fat guy next to him, is Burglas, our cook-steward. He's from Port-Said, but he cooks up a dream, the rascal!"

The fat bloke was dark-skinned, fat-lipped, weighed 130 kilos, had just a few scattered, yellow teeth, but was smiling wholeheartedly. Mario shook his hand. "Nice to meet you, my friend, but Burglas sounds Greek somehow..."

The fatty opened his mouth in an attempt to respond, but turned to Charis for assistance. Charis laughed. "His real name's Mohammad. We nicknamed him Burglas because he wants us to call him by a Greek-sounding name."

"But why Burglas?"

"Because of his previous career. He used to be a thief in Egypt. A cat burglar."

"A cat burglar so overweight?"

"Poor bloke, he used to be thin when he'd started out his career, but he was hooked on nosh. He ate like a horse and gained so much weight, he couldn't 'work' any more. So he was forced to turn his obsession into a profession, and here he is!"

He slurped the last sip from his drink, refilled it, and stood up.

"Listen up! We are loading tomorrow and heading off to Malta to wait there. Franco has already left for Italy to make arrangements with the squadra."

"We'll be waiting in Malta without a cargo attendant? We haven't done this since before you, Charis."

"I know, Makis, but there's no other way. They're having trouble either with the post or the speedboat coxwain—I'm not sure—but they're not ready yet. One thing's for certain: we'll be working Sicily again, so I thought it better to be closer by. Unless you guys prefer to stay here."

The young man from Corfu raised his glass. "My darling, Valetta, here I come!"

CHAPTER 4

With armed soldiers overseeing the procedure, the loading started early in the morning and lasted till ten o'clock at night, the Salonica had its guts filled with twenty-five thousand boxes. It cleared with the authorities pretty easily and set sail for the south with a full moon overhead and a calm sea as flat and glassy as a mirror. The Corfiot approached Mario, wiping his hands with a dirty rag.

"We're done. Let's go upstairs."

"Upstairs where?"

"The bridge, Mario. Where else? We've finished, let's get a drink."

"Do you have drinks on the bridge, Spyros?"

The Corfiot burst out laughing. "Oh, of course, I forgot. For you of the merchant navy, something like this is inconceivable. But here things are different, Mario. We spend almost all our spare time on the bridge."

"Why not in the lounge, which is more comfortable and bright?"

"Because the more of us watching outside, the better. Come on, let's go."

Phaedo was steering silently, with his body still like a statue and the moonlight illuminating the bridge, which made his craggy face look even uglier. The captain felt the draft from the door opening and raised his head from the radar. "Bon voyage, dudes! Phaedo, keep steady 180 knots for an hour. How has it been, Mario? What do you make of the ship up close?"

"It's fine. Not so much from the outside, but inside, it's a beauty."

The engineer entered the bridge with Burglas, the cook, who was carrying a tray of mixed nuts.

"Come on in, Makis. What's happening with the electricity engine? Is it going to get us through?"

"No, problem, it's as good as new." While speaking, Makis pulled out a bottle from the box behind the wheel and looked around him. "Where are the tumblers, you Burglas? Have you only remembered the mixed nuts?"

The fatty also looked around and pointed toward Phaedo.

"I give him glasses. Where dey are, Phaedo?"

Phaedo replied slowly, with bullying derision. "I left them downstairs, you fatso! Are you going to tell me off now or what?"

"Ok, Phaedo. Dis no problem."

"Fuck no problem, you fatty! Are you in charge too now? Go on then; go get them from downstairs, to exercise your fat ass a little."

Burglas put his head down without answering, opened the door, went outside, and Charis exploded. "For the last time, how's it going to be with you, wanker? Can you tell me what's come over you and why you're angry with everyone? I've warned you, but you you're not changing your tune. Are you disrespecting me, Phaedo? Because I can definitely do better. Are you following me? Go off now and get some sleep. Mario, grab the wheel, please, and keep 180."

Mario approached Phaedo, who neither answered nor moved from his spot. "Let go, mate. I'll take over."

"Why? Are you better at steering?"

Mario made an exhausted grimace. "Look, mate, I'm not here to play games with you. I'm here to make a pile. Settle your differences and your rage with those that have harmed you. All right? Let go of the helm now."

Without budging from his place, Phaedo flicked his cigarette ash to the floor, then turned to Mario, and blew the smoke in his face. "It's chock-full of captains in here."

Mario smiled, and Phaedo, who took that as a sign of weakness, laughed ironically. "Go eat a hazelnut or two to beef up. My treat."

Still smiling, Mario looked at him for a second, shook his head, and headed for the door.

"As you wish, mate."

Mario's spinning was swift. With an open palm, his left hand landed with power on Phaedo's ear, while with his right he pulled Phaedo's hand off the wheel, turning and twisting it behind his back. Phaedo was propelled, knocking his side on the telegraph, losing his balance, and landing on his knees by the door, exactly when Burglas was coming back in with a heap of plastic glasses. Fatty tripped on Phaedo but managed to stay standing, whereas the plastic cups got away and scattered. Phaedo got up with difficulty, fumbled about his waist looking for something, stared daggers at Mario, and waved his fist threateningly.

"You inbred! You faggot!"

Mario immediately plunged to grab him, but Phaedo was quick to close the door and position his body against it. With their mugs stuck on the shatter-proof, double-glazed panel, they were pushing the door, one to open it and the other to keep it shut, while the captain with the Corfiot's assistance managed to pull Mario away. "That's enough, Mario. It's over!"

Mario let them push him away and gave Phaedo a look, who, with his finger on his throat, was signalling that he was going to cut Mario's head off.

"I'm getting rid of the bastard in Valetta. I've had enough of him!" the Captain shouted.

"Why does he have it in for me, Captain Charis? Do you know anything?"

"I don't think he has it in especially for you. He's always been loopy, but since we got to Plotche, it's been over the top. I've asked him ten times to tell me what the matter is, but the nutter won't say a word. In any case, just to be on the safe side, keep your wits about until we reach the port."

It was almost midnight, the moon moved on to the stern, and the sea was calm. Makis and Fatty went to bed downstairs and there were only three left on the bridge, drinking and observing the ocean. Charis filled his glass again and looked at the clock on the bridge.

"That's the last one for today. I think I'm going to get a little rest. We've got a clear horizon, but if you need me, wake me up immediately. Keep your eyes open to avoid any surprises."

"What kind of surprises?"

"Whatever you can think of; just be careful."

"Aren't we in international waters?"

"There is no such thing for us. This is contraband and if—" He stopped abruptly and stared at the door. Mario and the Corfiot, who followed his gaze, barely made out Phaedo's silhouette, before the shadow lowered, in order to hide.

"What are you doing here, you nutter? Haven't I told you to go to bed?" Charis ordered.

The shadow moved a little, but didn't walk away. Charis headed for the door in a hostile mood, but Mario stepped in front of him and stopped him.

"Leave him, Captain Charis. It's no big deal. Come along, Phaedo, let's have a drink. Come in, join us. I'm not holding any hard feelings. Don't worry about it."

Nothing happened for a while, and then the shadow moved slowly, the door half-opened, and Phaedo stared at Mario in disbelief. Mario went back to the helm and picked up the glass he had laid by the compass.

"Come on, take mine to have a drink. The rest on the floor are a mess."

Charis moved aside to let him pass, while he observed him closely.

"Eh you, are you OK? Has the madness subsided?"

With his eyes stuck on Mario, Phaedo walked carefully and stretched his left hand to get the glass Mario had offered him, while with the right he was holding his back. He took the glass reluctantly and held it high between them.

"Where are you going to drink from?" Phaedo asked, hesitating.

"We'll drink from the same glass, you Phaedo. Don't worry, I'm clean."

With a shaky hand and a face in utter confusion, Phaedo twirled the glass around and mumbled something no one understood.

"What did you say?"

Phaedo looked embarrassed at the captain and the Corfiot, who had been watching him in silence, cleared his throat, and turned his attention at the plastic cup again.

"Aren't you angry, though?" Mario insisted.

"Come on, I've told you; I'm fine. Besides, I doubt that you meant the bullshit you said, because we haven't got any differences. Am I right?"

Totally perplexed, Phaedo turned to the plastic cup again looking for an answer, so Charis, who approached him smiling, helped him out of the awkward situation. "The madness has passed, you nutter, hasn't it? Well then, since you didn't feel like sleeping, you two stay here and see through the shift together. Let's go to bed, you little Corfiot."

They were left alone on the bridge and no one said anything for a few minutes. The moon dipped even lower on the stern, thickening the shadows and the sob cut through the monotonous drone of the engine. Mario, in disbelief, lifted his eyes from the compass and tried to make out Phaedo in the half-light. "What's the matter, mate? Are you crying?"

The sob was repeated stronger and Mario rushed down from the helm to investigate what was going on. "You are actually crying! Why, Phaedo? Is it my fault?"

There was no more room for Phaedo to draw back and hide, so he covered his face with his hands and sank in the corner.

"No, Mario. You're all right. It's my fault."

"It's no big deal, bro. Don't be like that. We've all cocked up. We don't take it to heart!" He grabbed Phaedo from his shoulders and forced him to raise his head, so he could look straight at him. "You realized that you've screwed up and came back, so there's really no offense, Phaedo. Everything's cool."

Looking down on the floor with his wet eyes, Phaedo talked slowly. "You don't understand, Mario."

"Don't understand what?"

"I didn't come back to make amends."

"What then?"

"I turned back to cut you. That's how much of a dick I am."

"What was that? To cut me? Why?"

Phaedo sighed deeply, with his eyes perpetually stuck on the floor. "I couldn't do it with my fists. I went downstairs to get a knife."

"Sure, but you took too long, didn't you? Which means you changed your mind."

"I didn't change my mind, I was just waiting for the others to leave the bridge."

"You came up, though, when Charis was still here with the Corfiot."

"I couldn't wait any longer, I was insanely furious."

"And you suddenly calmed down? Are you kidding me?"

The sob shook him again, and his eyes filled with tears. "You invited me in, Mario. I was expecting you to pounce at me and you offered me your drink. No one has ever treated me like this before. Forgive me, brother..."

Mario stared at him, baffled, patted him on the back, and took him by the arm. "You're forgiven, dude, if that's how you want it! Besides, it's no big deal. Come along here now, closer to the helm, to help stay on course, because we're circumnavigating."

He sat him down on the stool beside him and turned the wheel to bring the ship on course.

"You pour us drinks, Phaedo, and keep an eye on the stern until I steady it."

He reached for the glass, when it suddenly dawned on him. "By the way, what have you done with the knife? Have you thrown it away?"

Phaedo lifted his top and pulled from his back the double-edged stiletto that was gleaming menacingly in the moonlight. "I've got it right here!"

Mario swallowed the lump in his throat discreetly and attempted to sound as natural as possible. "And are you a master of it, Phaedo? Do you know how to use it?"

"From a very young age."

"Throw it over there, on the calendar, so I can see you."

Without even needing to adjust his body, Phaedo threw the blade over his shoulder. It landed on the throat of the naked babe posing for October. Mario filled up his drink and took a slurp to hydrate his throat, which dried up all of a sudden.

"That's really cool. I'm impressed!"

Phaedo looked at him, dejected. "What's the use, Mario? This brings only trouble. When everybody else was getting an education, I was studying the use of a stiletto."

"How'd that happen, mate?"

It took a few more drinks for Phaedo to start pouring his heart out to his new best friend, the same person he had planned to slash moments earlier. From orphanage to juvie, and from there on to prison, Phaedo used to drag his little sister around with him on the streets of Piraeus, since their mother was lost early and there'd never been a father. A soldier who'd messed badly with the young girl was stabbed in the spleen, but survived. Phaedo, though, had to spend four years in the can and by the time he was released, Mary, his little sister, had disappeared.

He had been in turmoil for six whole months, until he finally discovered her in a nightclub in Epirus, where the blade came in handy twice to get her out of trouble with the objecting panderers. Then, a distant aunt in Athens offered shelter to the young woman and promised to look after her. That's why Phaedo joined the contraband—to make a mint and help her set up the salon she'd been dreaming of, to have a job, earn her living.

Phaedo had been putting a little cash by, sending some to his little sister so that she wouldn't be a burden on their aunt, rang her every now and then, just to listen to her voice and give her strength. Last time, when he'd rang from Plotche, his aunt picked up and informed him, sobbing, that young Mary had disappeared again for the past ten days and that some acquaintance had told her that her niece was hooked on smack and turning tricks to score.

Phaedo fell silent and Mario, moved, squeezed his arm.

"How do you intend to fight this, mate? Just remember, I'm here for you in any way I can."

Phaedo's weeping shuddered his whole body.

CHAPTER 5

Conforming to their agreement, some years ago the English colonizers packed up, loaded their vessels and left Malta, leaving the natives overjoyed, dancing and having firework displays in the wharf, celebrating their independence. The hard times hit the Maltese after the festivities ended and they pulled out the drawers to pay the bill. Not used to exerting themselves, they ran into difficulties, got a headache, and fell into hard thought, trying to figure out how to refill their drawers and shipshape things. A difficult feat, indeed, since the English, on their way out, took back with them not only the crème de la crème of centuries and whatever they could fit into their ships, but also their technocrats with their systems and, what's worse, their sole source of income, tourism.

One of the easiest solutions to their problems was to slacken the constraints of morals and permit the docking of all sorts of contraband ships, from around the world, in

Valetta, with very few questions and even fewer formalities involved.

The Salonica moored below the medieval castle and next to five more contrabands, Makis remained on board to regulate his engines and guard the cargo, whereas the rest started treading uphill, cursing, since the enormous lift in place for this purpose had ceased operating ages ago—the first casualty of desertion.

One of the last constructions of the colonists, the hotel, was of modern architecture and clean. The people working there were extremely polite and smiling. Mario thanked a young employee for the information by placing a five-dollar bill in his palm. The young lad informed him that he could depend on him for anything he required, winked knowingly, and showed him to Charis's room. He found him there combing his hair in front of the mirror, all dressed up, in a very good mood, ready to go, singing like a tuneless Parios.

"Are you going out so early?"

Charis looked at him through the mirror, astonished. "Is this your first time to Malta?"

"Yes."

"Now it makes sense, 'cuz if you'd been here before, you wouldn't be asking this question."

"Are you going to fill me in?"

"Here, lad, the ladies are much more numerous than the men. They are plentiful and lonely. Are you following me? Why not put a hand in to counteract the imbalance? Did they not teach you in secondary school about the sense of justice of the Greeks? Shall we let the poor women suffer? Lose face with our ancestors?"

"So, in order not to ridicule ourselves in front of our ancestors, we're to forget all about work and shag Maltese women? What are we going to do with the cargo?"

Charis, laughing, repositioned carefully an unruly tuft of his hair, checked out his backside, purred with satisfaction, and turned to Mario. "Don't rush, mate. You're even worse than the Maltese ladies! Try to have some fun, because we'll spend a week here. Are you following me? I've just had a call from the Italians. The post will be ready next Monday. The day after tomorrow, Franco, the cargo attendant, will be joining us as well. Remember him?"

"And what'll we be doing for a whole week? Sitting around?"

"You can do whatever you please. If you're not up for games, go back to the ship. You'll always find something to do there, to kill your time."

"And work on my own? I'm not that crazy!"

"See? Now, if you want to come along, get ready quickly, I'll be waiting for you at the bar."

"It's been spot-on, hasn't it, dude?"

Mario averted his gaze from the small islands of Malta that were fading away into the horizon and turned around, absent-minded. "What has, Phaedo?"

"I'm just saying, we've had a brilliant week."

Mario smiled and patted him amicably on the back. For Phaedo, the ripper, everything was cool now, since he managed to contact his little sister Mary and relieve the burden on his soul. He'd spent the first twenty-four hours in Malta trying to get in touch with her, with the telephone in his lap. Finally he located her through a friend and young Mary rang him the following day from their aunt's to sugarcoat him, and she succeeded. So Phaedo's tempestuous soul calmed down, he found his old self again, and while he cruised down Straight Street to celebrate, he ran into Mario and Charis, and from that moment on, stuck to them like glue. Lively and in good spirits, he convinced them to let him look after them and make up for his behaviour. He dragged them to dodgy places, introduced them to quite a few scoundrels, brought them the cream of the ladies available in Valetta, and did his best to make them feel like the lords of the manor. And he certainly pulled it off.

Franco, who arrived from Italy to accompany the cargo, joined the posse. The days went by in relentless binging, the week ended, and on Monday morning, with eyes red from lack of sleep, they set off for Sicily to make it to the post by late afternoon.

The day became grey, and the cloudy sky gradually turned the possibility of rain into certainty, the wind picked up, and the waves that had been lashing against the ship's starboard side were sending the raindrops forcefully on their mugs. Mario licked the saltiness from his lips and followed with his eyes an ore-carrier that was sailing calmly about half a mile off their bow, on route to Gibraltar. He rubbed his arms with his palms. "It's cold, Phaedo. Let's go to the bridge."

With one hand pinching hazelnuts from a bowl and the other steadying the binoculars in his eyes, Charis was inspecting the sea. Makis was gaping at the radar screen and the Corfiot was whining by the helm. "Just some soup, Captain Charis. A little soup. It won't take longer than five minutes. It won't be the end of the world if we stop for five minutes."

Charis kept a hazelnut hovering in front of his mouth and answered, irritated, without turning around. "It's not about the five minutes, you dimwit. We might get into trouble."

"It won't be the first time we've stopped for fish. Have we ever got into trouble before? They'll trade us some fresh fishies to make a soup for some cigarettes, and that's it. Big deal!"

"No way am I stopping for them. There's something dodgy about them."

Mario put down the spare binoculars and examined carefully the fast sailing boat that was approaching, pinching against the weather.

"What's the matter, Captain Charis? It's just a fishing boat."

"Think a little, Mario. The wind is constantly picking up. If they were Sicilian fishermen, they would be rushing back to find shelter. What are they doing instead? They are defying the weather, bending over backwards to catch up with us, simply to get two boxes of cigarettes? They'll spend more on fuel. Are you following me? That's why I don't like them."

"And if they're not fishermen, what are they?"

"Jumpers, lad, pirates, but we'll know for certain in a little while."

The bloke, who appeared right at that moment on the fish boat's deck, was struggling to stay standing, screaming like a maniac and waving a fish, which looked like a bonito. Charis turned around, opened a drawer, and stuck his hand inside, searching.

"What did I say, you wanker Corfiot. They're pirates."

The Corfiot looked at him, bewildered. "But the man is not holding a sabre, Charis. He's holding a fish..."

Charis found the forty-five he'd been looking for in the drawer, checked it out quickly, laid it on the shelf in front of him, and took the binoculars again.

"They're shameless! They haven't even sacrificed a crate of fish. They're trying to entice us with just the one fish!"

"Are you sure, Charis?"

The captain ignored the Corfiot, put the binoculars aside, and addressed the engineer. "Makis, I want full revs. Now!"

"OK, Charis, but there aren't that many."

"As many as there are! I want flank speed. Get out of here quickly!"

He looked at Makis, who got out running, and turned to the others. "Well, dudes, pay attention. These thugs haven't revealed themselves yet because they think we'll swallow the bait and stop. As soon as they realise that we're not falling for it, they'll try to jump on board."

"Take it easy, Charis! Who's gonna jump, anyway? That poor bloke with the bonito? Ram-raiding with a bonito?"

Charis approached the helm really cross and shook the Corfiot, who was guffawing so hard, he was losing his breath. "Pull yourself together, you idiot, and listen to me! Point up slowly, so that they can't accost, and when I say so, start shifting the helm twenty degrees right, twenty left—always weatherboard—but without stability. Oi, are you following me?"

The Corfiot, still surprised, glanced at Mario and Phaedo, who had been listening solemnly, and nodded. "Done, Captain Charis. Whatever you say."

"Keep your eyes open. It's in our interests not to let them jump on the ship. As long as they stay on the sailing boat, they can't do much, but if they get on board, we've had our chips!"

He brought the binoculars to his eyes again and continued watching the sailing boat, which had drawn near, at around fifty metres.

"I'll go and talk to them, in case they go away without any trouble. In the meantime, Phaedo, hurry to wake up Franco, and ask him to bring his gun, so you can guard the gunwale together as they're approaching. Warn Burglas as well, to drop his pots and pans and come out. I want us to seem like a big group. Hurry!"

"Shall I go down with them?"

"No, Mario, I'll need you right here."

He threw the gun in his pocket and went out to the port side. Dancing on the waves, the sailing boat reached a ten-metre distance and attempted to stay on parallel course with the ship. The bloke spotted Charis on the wing, dropped the fish at his feet, cupped his palms and started calling out.

Charis cupped his hands too and replied, but the other got cross, waved the fish again, so Charis had to repeat himself. The bloke suddenly got really wild and flung the fish away, cursing.

The fish hit the ship's hull and disappeared in the water.

"What are they saying, Spyros? Are you getting anything?"

"He wants us to stop, to sell us fish."

"And Charis?"

"Charis told him we don't need fish, so he won't be stopping."

Scared to death, the helmsman turned backward to buy some time to get away. He made it, but the Salonica's stern hit the water just one metre away from the caïque, filling it with water, sweeping the brute away and thrusting him down. Knowing that he might not have another chance, the helmsman went at full throttle, turned a little to the right, then sharply to the left, precisely at the moment when the Salonica came splashing down, at the spot where, three seconds earlier, his boat had been positioned.

Mario was certain that the pirates would give up after that, but he was sadly mistaken. Lying in water, the thug found his gun and, wailing like a maniac, started shooting blindly, emptying the cartridge. One of the bullets got to the bridge, pierced the bulkhead, and was lodged a few centimeters below the clock, adjacent to the Corfiot, who changed color, abandoned the helm, and became one with the floor.

Charis rushed in and kicked him on the side.

"Get out of here, you punk. Join the others downstairs. Ram-raiding with a bonito, eh, you wanker! Mario, grab the helm and stay weatherly. If they go for it again, you know, first right then left, let's not go over this again."

With his mouth wide open from fear, the Corfiot took a look at the hole left behind by the bullet and slipped away, crawling, without reason anymore, since, in the meantime, the sailing boat reduced its speed and was left about two hundred metres behind. Charis went out to the port side again.

"Is everyone all right? Good, but stay put, because they might pounce on us again unexpectedly."

"What are they doing now, Captain Charis?"

Charis was watching through the binoculars the pirates arguing on the fish boat's deck.

"A meeting, Mario. They're having a meeting to decide if they can take on another attempt."

"What do you think? Are they going to try again?"

"I think so, because they're running out of time."

"Why? Aren't we in the middle of the ocean? They can go for it again whenever they fancy."

"That's not the case. In about two hours, we'll be able to speak with our guys ashore and they know that. Whatever they have to do, it must be fast. Are you following me?"

"I'm following you, Captain, but I don't understand. What's going to happen if we communicate with our men? Are they going to get scared? They're not even afraid of God, the way they're armed to the teeth."

Despite the cracking tension, Charis laughed. "They might not be scared of God, but they're terrified of Signorino."

"Why, who's that?"

"He's in charge of the cargo and the squadra. If he goes after them, he's going to cut them to pieces and make an example of them."

"Is he so tough that...how'd you call him? Signorino?"

Charis released the binoculars with one hand to shake the dust off his collar.

"Don't call him Signorino, because he gets mad. Are you following me? Call him Vincenzo. That's his real name."

"And Signorino, where does it come from? Isn't it his name?"

"It's his nickname. We only use it when he's not around. I told you. He gets really annoyed."

"Agreed, but why wait to speak to Signorino and not notify the coastguard, to bang them up and get it over with?"

"They won't bang them up, Mario. We'll go down instead. Have you forgotten already the business we're in?"

"They'll get us and not the pirates? That sounds crazy. What the hell, this is not the Middle Ages."

"Did you see how they were revving up earlier? Their entire hold fits the engine. They're difficult to catch, and even if they could, they'd still go after us."

"Why is that?"

"Let's say they've arrested and dubbed up four scums. What's the big deal? Nothing. Whereas, if the bring us down, they'll pile it in. They get commission from the confiscated goods. Which means big money, so don't dream of help from…"

He stopped speaking and stretched out to get a better view.

"Here they come! Start the maneuvers."

He pulled his gun and darted outside to give instructions to the rest of the crew, who had formed a huddle on the deck. Roaring and jumping from wave to wave, the pirate ship, in full speed, was getting ready to attack again from the port side. The brute had moved forward to the bow and was lying on his face aiming at the ship, while the young jumpers, who had no reason to hide any more, balanced their bodies, holding on to the rigging with one hand and to their guns—all set, barrels high—with the other.

Half-bent on the gunwale and extremely tense, the Salonica's crew was waiting for the second attack, squeezing in their hands the tools they'd been holding to defend themselves. Franco fired the first shot with the Berretta, aiming at the fishing boat's helmsman, precisely when Mario was turning full to the left for the first maneuver. The maneuver changed the ship's position, making Franco miss, his bullets scattered in the sea, but saving Mario and Charis, since the thug's shot meant for them went astray, wreaking havoc in the superstructure's mirror.

Revealing that this was the signal they'd been waiting for, the young lads began raking at the deck simultaneously, forcing the men to lower even more shield themselves. Mario saw the caïque reaching the spot where the men had been barricaded and prepared to start yelling to alert them. But the caïque didn't slow down and went past them heading for the bow. While the three pirates had been firing incessantly, Mario listed the ship to close them in, but, by the time the rudder obeyed, the sailing boat had doubled the bow and, for a moment, disappeared from his field of vision. Mario got confused, but not the old sea dog, Charis, who sprung up shouting.

"They're going to go for the other side, the other side! Everyone get starboard, quickly!"

Terrified and lost, the men raised their heads carefully searching for the caïque, wasting the time it took the pirate ship to draw alongside them.

"Starboard, quickly!"

Charis's cries boosted them and they reacted all together, with Makis, the engineer, being the swiftest, as he dove and tumbled like a commando, over the hold, getting there first. Shaped like a hook, the young pirate's palm was raised over the deck, looking for the right spot to hold on to and jump aboard. Behind him, the other young man secured the gun on his shoulder to free his hands and, further back, the thug kept firing nonstop for diversion.

With the bullets whizzing past his head, Makis approached, arched like a wildcat, precisely when the jumper's palm had fumbled its way into a convenient place and got a firm grasp. Makis lifted himself up as required and thrust the jemmy down forcefully.

The sound of broken bones and the young man's long, drawn-out, primal scream made them shudder. With his eyes bulging from the pain and his mouth wide open, the young pirate swayed, lost his balance, knocked his head on the hull and fell backwards, dragging his companion overboard. Mouthing curses, the helmsman turned back immediately. The thug looked around in confusion, threw his gun down, and plunged in to help the young man, while the other young man, with the smashed fingers, was left on his own on the deck, writhing in agony.

Cheering with excitement, Phaedo and the Corfiot climbed to the hold to celebrate the victory with Native American war dances. The fat cook was laughing, waving his cleaver threateningly towards the fading caïque, while Makis just about managed to pull Franco's hand down, who was aiming at the helmsman again.

"Basta, Franco. There's no need anymore."

Shaking with tension, Franco put his Berretta down. He had to force himself, but he smiled in the end. "Va bene, Makis, va bene."

Mario steadied the ship and, making sure he'd swallowed the lump in his throat, which had been troubling him for a while, asked, "What do we do know, Captain Charis?"

Charis, having made sure that the helmsman had collected his men from the sea, smiled satisfactorily, hung his binoculars on his chest, and looked at the bridge clock.

"Get back on route for the post. Maybe we can still make it."

CHAPTER 6

"There they are! They've finally found us!"

Mario approached quickly to follow Charis' outstretched hand that was indicating something three inches to the right of the bow. At first, he could only make out the spume from the wash, but then he was able to see three black dots, which were increasing in size, as they were drawing nearer. The wind had abated a while ago and it had briefly rained heavily. Then, the clouds became thinner, breaking through the darkness, but the mighty yet silent waves kept splashing on their side, giving them a hard time.

They'd reached the pre-arranged position while it was still raining, but due to the two-hour delay on account of the pirates, they'd found no boats waiting for them. They set up short lookouts on the flying bridge, calling them with walkie-talkies from a height, but an hour later they were all soaking wet and no speeding boats in sight. Charis gathered them all at the bridge.

"Look, the lads may have turned back, since they couldn't find us at the meeting point. They may well be still looking for us, but we can't hang around here for much longer, as we're just thirty miles away from the shore and we're in danger of being detected."

"Good, let's head out thirty more miles and get some sleep. Tomorrow is a new day."

With his back stuck in the corner to keep steady, Phaedo agreed with the Corfiot, without distracting his attention from the nails he was tending to with the stiletto.

"He's right, Charis; tomorrow is another day. How long should we keep looking for them? That fucking roll has wrecked us, we haven't even eaten today."

"Me no fault, no food. Moving much, no..."

The captain gesticulated impatiently. "No, worries, Burglas. No one said it's your fault. I assume, though, that you agree with them, right?"

From the floor, where he'd been sitting for security, the fat cook nodded longingly.

"What do you say, Makis?"

"I say that, since we're already at the designated spot, we should be patient for a couple more hours. You never know."

Charis stopped the Corfiot's nagging with a killer look and explained the situation to Franco, who was following the conversation intently, but without understanding much. The Italian listened to Charis carefully and then declared that he would stand by the captain's decision, fixing himself again to the telegraph pole to avoid falling.

The wave that hit their side at that precise moment was bigger than the rest, and the Salonica lifted, creaking. Glasses and dry food flew off Phaedo's corner and swung back with force. The Corfiot caught the salami travelling on the floor, looked at it in disgust, opened the door, and threw it in the sea.

"Charis, we can't keep this up. Make a decision and get it over with. The roll is going to finish us."

"It's just you left, Mario. It's a tie, three all."

"I don't know what to say, Captain Charis. I'm new here. How should I know?"

"I'll explain it, it's simple. If you vote for continuing the search, we'll sail one hour to the west, and if we don't find them, we'll turn back two hours to the east. Are you following me? We'll be calling them out, like before, in short lookouts. At least it's not raining any more. Do you get it now? It's up to you."

Mario put aside the Corfiot, who stood in his way to influence him and avoided Burglas's imploring look. "Yes, I'd rather we kept searching..."

The Salonica was situated five miles west from the assigned position. The first deadline was due to end with Phaedo's watch, who, as soon as he got up to the flying bridge to take over, started yelling. "Come here, Charis! Hurry, I can hear something!"

A few minutes later, Charis went downstairs pleased and patted Mario on the back.

"Thank God, you voted wisely. Signorino is with them."

Mario felt envious as the speedboats performed a swift, flashy circle around them in greeting and waited for the Salonica to cut its speed.

Then, one of them approached while the rest kept their distance and had their engine caps opened for the requisite inspection before the return voyage.

Charis rang SLOW on the engine order telegraph and gave the helmsman instructions.

"So, Mario, bring your bow gently leeward. And keep steady there."

"Are we going to stop?"

"It's not possible. The wave is heavy and they'll be in danger of breaking up on us."

"But, aren't they going to load?"

"We'll load them in motion."

The bloke standing upright on the speedboat's bow reached out his hand to catch the rope ladder, but was forced to pull it back, as the ship was listing dangerously. Remaining cool, he turned his head toward the operator and signalled him to try again.

Mario was able make out the speedboat wheelman, who was manoeuvring nimbly, so he chose the right moment and approached gently.

The bloke on the bow grabbed the rope ladder and climbed onboard as easily as an acrobat.

"Is that Signorino?"

Charis turned around abruptly, biting his lip. "Remember what we said; don't let it slip in front of him, because his gets really cross. His name's Vincenzo, keep that in mind."

"Why is he here? Is he going to travel with us?"

"No, of course not, but sometimes he likes to inspect the business when it's starting out. We may see him again, after we've finished, maybe not."

Panting from over-trying, fatty Burglas opened the door with his elbow. He was carrying a jug of hot coffee and a bottle of cognac that Charis had requested earlier.

Signorino, who just appeared behind him, moved to help him. The fatty politely refused, bowed his head with respect and shifted his mass to make room for him to pass. Further behind, Franco was following, visibly upset.

With panther-like movements and a little-over-average height, Vincenzo moved on to the bridge, threw his cap on a chair, and hugged Charis, who'd been expecting him. They kissed each other twice on both cheeks, without speaking. Then Charis told him something, he answered in one word, Charis kept talking, and, for the first time, the Italian turned his eyes to the wheel and noticed Mario.

Mario felt angry at himself for feeling nervous, but looked straight back at him, and when he read an expression resembling a smile, he smiled back.

For a few seconds, the Italian sized Mario up. Next, his smile widened, he got closer, and opened his arms. Agitated and surprised, Mario surrendered himself to the Italian's tight embrace, while the kisses on the cheeks were repeated. He heard a grazie and some bravos, but he couldn't understand and looked puzzled at his captain.

Charis laughed. "I told him that we found them because of you. They sweated blood searching for us for so many hours and they got extremely worried."

Holding Mario from his shoulders very brotherly, the Italian nodded his head quite pleased, and the young man managed to examine him more carefully in half-darkness.

Thirty-five years old—maximum forty—unshaven and exhausted, in a soaking and filthy wetsuit that was torn at the arm, it was everything that should make him look miserable and pathetic. It wasn't enough, however, to mar Signorino's strong personality and natural nobility. He had the grace of a man who was born a leader. His bright-green iron gaze was warm yet icy at the same time. In his hair, two white tufts were distinguishable, a golden chain that could tow a boat was hanging from his neck, and he sported a diamond ring the size of a hazelnut on his middle finger.

"Parla Italiano, Mario?"

Mario shook his head, disappointed. The Italian laughed wholeheartedly, mumbled something in his language, and Mario looked at the captain again questioningly.

"Don't you worry, he said, because, by his reckoning, you'll learn quickly."

Mario thanked him in Italian, which pleased Signorino, who felt his judgement was quickly vindicated, and he laughed. The laughter cut through the tension from the agitation and tiredness that had taken its toll on everyone, and, still laughing, Charis gave the necessary instructions to commence the loading procedure on the speedboats that were following the ship slowly, a short distance behind.

Phaedo and the Corfiot opened up the hold and suspended a row of old car tires on the side they would be unloading from. Afterward, they placed two inspection lamps on each corner to get light, and they formed a human chain from the hold to the deck with fatty Burglas and Franco, and they began passing on the boxes.

Mario was keeping steady, and the ship wasn't rolling much. Although its speed was no more than three knots per hour, it was quite difficult for the speedboats to approach safely.

Trying to stay within a distance no bigger than five metres from the ship, the first speedboat drew near and the human chain started throwing the crates toward it. For about thirty passes, things were moving along smoothly— then a box missed its target and fell overboard. The young speedboat driver's assistant almost fell over as well, but managed to fish it out with the hook. The same thing happened a little later when the kid didn't quite make it, but that time the box got lost in the dark.

Mario felt the youngster's worry and looked at Signorino, but he remained expressionless, as if he hadn't detected the loss.

Two more crates vanished in the water, until the boat was filled to capacity with 250 crates. Then it moved away to wait for the others.

They were luckier with the second speedboat, and only lost one box. It was a lengthy procedure, though, and the night was almost over, so Charis began biting his nails in anxiety.

At the last speedboat, the passes became more hasty and careless, the speedboat coxswain, due to mistaken calculations, hit the ship twice, and five more crates were lost. Signorino kept watching unruffled and equally expressionless, sipping his coffee slowly, without making any comments. They were passing the last boxes on when he got up, hugged Mario, spoke with Charis for about two minutes, kissed him, and went down the rope ladder.

The speedboat came as close as it could, Signorino jumped in, raised his hand waving, and the boats set off for the shore, engines roaring altogether, just as they did when they arrived.

Charis took a look at the radar, placed the telegraph on full speed ahead, and came out.

"Hurry, collect the fenders and the inspection lamps, and shut the hold. Mario, turn one 150 degrees, and we're out of here, because dawn's breaking, and we're not safe."

"But we're more than thirty miles off the shore. Do they patrol so far out?"

"I'm worried about the helicopters, as they can report us and lead the coastguard straight here. And even if we don't get caught, we won't be able to work here again, because they'll know the position. Which means damage. Are you following me? We'll move three hours away, sleep safely, and return at night."

Mario was silent for a moment, until he set his course on 150 degrees and then asked, pointing in the direction the speedboats had headed. "How about them, going out to shore? Isn't daybreak dangerous for them? Won't they be seen?"

"Their speed is close to forty miles, while ours is twelve, Mario. They're certainly in greater danger than us, since they're going out to the shore, but that's why they're getting the big pile."

"What if they get Signorino, who's with them now?"

"Signorino? Tough!"

"Why?"

"Because the man is not only sharp, but also has dosh on him."

"I didn't catch that, Captain Charis."

"Didn't you see the jewelery and the diamonds he's got on him? You must have noticed. The man is like a moving jewelery shop."

"So, what? They're going to respect him because he's got golden chains on? Are you kidding me?"

Charis looked over his shoulder, frowning.

"You haven't grasped it again, have you?"

"So, tell me..."

"Lad, depending on the seriousness of the situation, you hand the appropriate jewel to the person in charge, and off you go! Concentrated money, so to speak. Are you following me?"

"And it works?"

"Of course it works; they're public servants. They make so much more money this way, without formalities, and they're always busy, to account for their salary."

"What if you're skint and don't have any diamonds to oil the knocker? What happens then, are you going to be dubbed up?"

"In a flash. They confiscate the cargo, declare whatever they fancy, clean up their commission, but they also bang you up to set an example not to get involved in dodgy business if you're flat, because more laymen acquire bad habits, and it's not profitable for them."

The smell from the pot that the fatty was carrying reminded them that they hadn't eaten all day, and they interrupted the conversation. Wheezing as always, the fatty left the food with two bowls and went off to bed.

The horizon turned orange red in the sunrise, foreshadowing a beautiful day. The quiet mood began to fade and the two men, alone on the bridge, eating silently, recalled the pirates.

"What has Signorino told you about the raiders?" Mario searched, intrigued by everything he had witnessed.

"He's heard of them before, he said. It's a family. An idiot with his sons and his son-in-law from Palermo, usually attacking Libyan fishermen, only this time they went too far..."

"What's going to happen?"

"Whatever happens, their career ends here. There are certain rules. No one can do as he pleases."

"And who's going to go after them? Signorino?"

"Not necessarily. Thousands of people make a living from the contraband. They won't go out of business because of an abscess. They'll squeeze it, and that's it. Are you following me?"

"Is that why he didn't look cross?"

"He never makes his feelings known anyway. He liked you, though."

"Really? Why?"

"He's got something in mind, because he was asking me..."

Mario dropped the spoon and looked at him pensively. "How many people work for him, Captain Charis?"

"About 200..."

"And he was asking about me? What's wrong, Captain Charis? Do you suspect anything?"

It was Charis's turn to look at him ponderingly; then he got up and opened a drawer.

"Take this."

Mario looked at the book, confused.

"What should I do with Teach Yourself Italian, Captain Charis? I'm not up for foreign language learning! I'm only here to make a pile."

"Agreed, you're here to make some dosh, like the rest of us. But, think, if Signorino wants you for something, it's going to be tough without the language. Are you following me? Read that as much as you can and I'll help you, as well."

...

They set off for their position again in the afternoon, and at dusk the speedboats arrived normally, on time, bringing them fresh fruit and food. This time they loaded without any losses or problems and left, taking with them the cargo attendant, Franco.

"Why is he leaving?"

"Signorino's orders."

"Isn't he worried about his cargo anymore?"

"Evidently, he trusts us."

The following evening, the first coxswain in loading position delivered a letter from Signorino to Charis. Charis read through the sparse lines and was left staring at it, scratching his chin.

"What is it, Captain Charis? What does it say?"

The captain replied slowly, distracted, without raising his head, as if he was talking to himself. "He says he wants me to go out to have a word…"

"He must be crazy. Abandon us here and get ashore for a chat? You can't do this, Captain Charis."

With bewilderment embossed on his face, Charis sat down and began scratching his chin again. "'No matter what,' he says. 'It's urgent.'"

"Has this happened before?"

"Of course not!"

"I don't think you should go. We can't be left without a captain."

Charis looked at him very serious and showed him the piece of paper. "Do you know what he says? To leave you in charge."

Mario almost dropped his cup of coffee. "He might be bonkers after all! I can't…Why doesn't he tell you what he wants on the radio telephone?"

"Because other people will be able to listen in."

"How long does he need you for?"

"Only for tonight. I'll be back tomorrow evening."

"Could be worse, but still I couldn't possibly…"

"Hang on, Mario, don't be rash, it could easily be done. The weather is OK, and, according to the forecast, tomorrow is going to be the same. It won't drag you very far. Are you following me? I'll set out the course that you'll need, and if you don't find me, I will find you."

"That means you've decided to go."

"I have to."

His stomach was tight as a fist from the dread of the huge responsibility he'd taken on, as he was watching his captain standing on the speedboat, waving goodbye. He tried to put on a brave face, so as not to betray his true state in front of the men.

He was impressed by the composure with which the crew had accepted this development, when Charis, just before he jumped on the speedboat, had gathered them to explain the situation. Not even the Corfiot had reacted, when he told them that Mario would be in charge till he was back, and was really moved when the tough, craggy mugs nodded in all seriousness, showing him their trust.

"Mario, just remember one thing. Your eyes. Are you following me? You'll be a captain as long as they don't see fear in your eyes."

Then he jumped on the boat. Mario took a last look on the boats, as they were making their way through the dark horizon, and smiled too. All of a sudden, he was overwhelmed by the sense that something major was going to happen in his life. He was no longer impressed when he casually headed for the telegraph to give instructions to Makis about the revs, not even when he had to try to make his voice sound natural.

"Lads, we're done for tonight. Pack it up, and let's go. Spyros, keep 210 degrees for the time being, and you, Burglas, bring us something to eat when you're ready."

With a calm sea and no incidents, a little after midnight and about sixty miles on the northeast of Sicily, he requested for the engine to be put on dead slow, he arranged for the young Corfiot, Spyros, to be on the second shift and left Phaedo to watch out the horizon. Afterward, he looked very carefully at the radar to ensure there were no other ships near them, took his little Italian book, and went downstairs to lie down.

Feeling more pleasant without the engine's roaring, with only the noise of the waves splashing on the hull in his ears, Mario reclined fully to relax, opened his book, and...fell asleep.

Used to being jolted in his sleep, he was annoyed but didn't wake up and rolled over to his other side. Lighting his face with the flashlight, the Corfiot shook him again. "Wake up, Mario!"

Mario opened his eyes, startled, and tried to push the blinding light away with is hand. "What, what is it?"

"Shh, Mario, be quiet."

He was whispering, and when he lowered his flashlight, Mario could see he was shaking.

"What's wrong, Spyros? Is there another ship close by?"

The Corfiot gulped.

"There's nothing passing by, but something is happening. I couldn't take it any longer, so I woke you up."

"What's going on, Spyros? Why are we whispering?"

"I don't know, Mario. I can hear something."

"Like what?"

"I don't know, I'm telling you. It's been going on for half an hour. At first I thought I was imagining it, but it's getting stronger."

"And you can't understand what it is?"

"No, I can't. I thought I'd wake you first, but I'm not sure if I should wake up the others, too."

"Let's go together first, so I can have a listen as well."

Switching on the flashlight only when necessary, they left the companionway and climbed carefully the external ladder, flexible like cats, with their ears taut.

Lowered and back-to-back to cover both directions, they took cover on the darkest side of the bridge, and Mario grabbed his arm. "Where, Spyros? I can't hear a thing..."

With the finger to his mouth, the Corfiot motioned him to stop talking. Mario held his breath to hear better and on exhaling was preparing to swear at him for waking him up for no reason, when his ears attuned to the sound, and he shivered all over.

By the time he'd classified it in his mind, the sound was gone again and Mario realized why the Corfiot thought he'd been imagining it. He got ready to speak, but Spyros stopped him again. "Wait, listen..."

The sound was heard again, lasted a few seconds, and vanished again. Mario sat up carefully and stretched his body to listen, scanning around the dark sea with his eyes. Then he motioned the Corfiot to get up and put a hand to his ear.

"It sounds close."

"What is it, Mario? Does it remind you of anything?"

The sound recurred stronger this time, there was something morbid about it, like a moan or a rale, fading like a sob and sending chills down their spines.

"That way, the port side."

Shaking, with eyes wide open, the Corfiot pulled him from the sleeve.

"What is it, Mario?"

The moaning continued even stronger with tormenting intervals, numbing Mario's back.

"I don't know yet, Spyros. Bring the binoculars."

He struggled to see something in the dark, but failed.

"Fuck, I can't see anything. What time is it?"

"Half-five."

"Luckily, it'll be dawn soon. Wake the engineer up to prepare the engine and then the rest. Tell them to be dead quiet and not to switch any lights on."

Three minutes later, they all crowded together, looking at each other in despair. Mario beckoned to them not to speak and drew closer to Makis, who was listening to the sounds with his mouth half-open.

"Is the engine ready?"

"The engine? Yes, it's all set. What's this thing, Mario?"

"I suspect something, but I'm not sure, so it's better to be prepared. Can I use the floodlight without starting the electricity engine?"

"Only for two or three minutes."

"That's good, as long as we see what the hell it is. Besides, dawn will be breaking soon. I'll go upstairs to switch it on, and all of you stay quiet and on standby, in case we have to set off quickly."

The moaning heard at that moment was so strong that it made Makis moisten his lips, frightened. Mario climbed quietly the steep, iron ladder, got out, removed the plastic cover, and grabbed the floodlight with both hands. He waited until he heard the sound again, aimed toward it, and flicked the switch. The artificial light tore through the night, revealing only a calm sea, and then Mario moved it slowly to the left, illuminating a mass, which looked like a small, black island.

Nothing happened for a few moments, then the mass stirred and the huge whale, terrified of the uninvited sun, stopped snoring and went under quickly, rippling the serene waters.

They started joking around to forget the fright they'd taken. They filled their glasses to the rim with whiskey and they all drank at six o'clock in the morning, at the time when the cetacean was re-surfacing about three hundred metres further to get back to sleep.

"Shall we go after the bitch?"

"Why, Spyros? Because she was sleeping?"

Spyros, annoyed, turned to confront Phaedo, who was giving him the finger.

"Fine, she was asleep. But did you know, you nutter, that whales snore when they're sleeping?"

Half an hour later they'd finished the bottle. It was morning by now, but they envied the whale's carefreeness, so they went downstairs to continue their sleep.

The mammal was going around near them, eating and blowing water high, until the afternoon, when it was time for them to set off again. It was swimming in all directions, always close to them, sensing it was not in danger, brazen and playful. When the engines started, though, it went down immediately and they didn't see it coming back up until they'd reached a significant distance.

The meeting was immaculate. Mario had the ship on the position right on time, and Charis, with his experience, led the speedboats there easily, like they were going on an excursion.

They'd just become visible, and the Corfiot threw the binoculars away and started celebrating, kissing Phaedo on the cheek, who wiped it with his sleeve in disgust. "What's wrong, young Spyros? Are you swinging both ways now? Africa is close by, you know. Why don't you pop in to get sorted?"

Still jumping with excitement, the Corfiot looked at him in disdain.

"Open your peepers, you wanker! Did you think I kissed you because you're handsome? Six speedboats are on their way!"

Astonished, Phaedo turned around eagerly, exclaimed something, and raised his fist triumphantly. Makis, quite pleased himself, attempted to explain all the jubilation to Mario, who didn't understand.

"This, my friend Mario, means that we'll finish very quickly. If the good weather lasts a little longer, next week we're done, and off we go to start afresh."

As it was customary, the Corfiot and Phaedo rushed to welcome them with the Native American dancing in the hold. Charis, who arrived as head of the fleet, upright on the bow, stood to attention and saluted them like an admiral, returning the honours, while his chest was shaking from laughter. He climbed aboard, chuckling still, greeted them one by one, gave them instructions to start working, and went upstairs to the bridge.

Mario, who'd been waiting for him by the door, feigned seriousness, whistled a military salute, and reported to his senior.

"Captain, Sir, welcome, and I beg to report that your ship is the same wreck as you remember it. I would like to request that I'm never laden with it again, so we can remain friends."

Charis hugged him, laughing, and dragged him inside.

"Come on, let's have a drink, because it was freezing on the boat. I have news that will probably interest you."

Mario propped his legs where he was standing. "I don't suppose you'll be leaving again?"

Charis failed to keep the bottle steady from all the chuckling and spilled the whiskey on the floor.

"I don't know if I'm leaving again, but you certainly are."

Mario froze. "Are you serious? You're giving me the boot already?"

Charis took a deep breath trying to control his laughing fit and managed to fill his glass.

"Don't you worry. The exact opposite is happening. You're being promoted."

He turned to look at Mario, who was looking at him rather lost, and burst out laughing again.

"Come, take a glass, and I'll tell you all about it."

Mario sat down in a trance, and Charis started telling him about Signorino, who got really cross the other night when he discovered with his own eyes that the speedboat navigators he's been using are useless.

"Useless? I thought they were all right."

"Maybe they're not completely useless, but the eight miles they missed us by are a lot and that's bad for business because we waste time looking and get exhausted going back and forth foolishly. Are you following me? Well, he never quite believed me that his coxswains got frequently lost, but the other night he witnessed it for himself, having a really hard time, so he got really cross and made the big decisions."

"What is he going to do? Get rid of all his speedboat drivers?"

"He's got something else in mind."

Charis explained that Signorino, wanting to increase his turnover, expanded to Napoli. He managed to find one more ship, but he had to deal with the problem of the delaying speedboat drivers, and the business wasn't running smoothly. That forced him to charter three more boats to clear this cargo and to be on the safe side in the future. But he also decided to build his own speedboat in Greece, of double capacity and faster, and to hire his own coxswain, solving the problem of delays once and for all.

Mario bolted upright and stooped with anticipation. "Have I been put forward for the coxswain's assistant position?"

Charis raised his glass. "Cheers, but you're not going to be an assistant. You're going to be the speedboat coxswain."

"Are you serious, Captain Charis? How?"

"It's simple, Mario. He despises the Italian speedboat wheelsmen. He wants to hire a Greek, and he liked you. So, he asked me, and I said that you'd love to work on a speedboat and that you'll definitely make it. Are you following me?"

"Go on..."

Charis got up to show him the speedboats below that continued loading.

"As soon as we're done with this cargo, we'll go to Durres to load a new one, which has already been paid for. Then we'll wait for about two months for the squadra to get organized and your boat to get ready. And...I'll miss you, you scamp."

"Why miss me? Won't I be unloading the Salonica again?"

"Yes, but I won't be here. She's going to get another captain. I'll be working at the other ship, in Napoli."

"Seriously? And we won't be seeing each other?"

"Maybe sometimes it coincides, but rarely, I imagine. If you weren't taking over the speedboat, I'd take you with me."

Having been bombarded with unexpected news, Mario was wondering if he was going to look immoral, sacrificing his friendship with Charis to work on a speedboat, though it had always been his dream.

"What do you think I should do, Captain Charis?"

An experienced man, Charis saw through him. "Grab the opportunity, Mario. Isn't that why you joined the contraband? You're asking me what to do, when you know I recommended you? Come on, get a grip."

Still feeling awkward, and trying to avoid his inexplicable guilt, Mario chose to change the subject. "Do you know the captain who's going to replace you here?"

"Certainly; I know him well. We've worked together for a long time. They call him Moustachy, man with a moustache, or Baffo—either is fine. He's an excellent captain, but completely bonkers..."

"That's bad. I don't see us getting along."

"No, you don't understand. Moustachy's madness is endearing. You can't argue with him. He means well, but he's just unpredictable. He's a nice bloke, though. Are you following me? You'll learn a lot from Moustachy because he's a competent sailor. But you've got to get cracking, to learn as much as possible and be ready. How are you getting on with Italian?"

Mario slowly lifted his eyes from the glass and looked at him. "What do you make of the situation, Captain Charis? Will I succeed? I don't even speak the language."

Charis ruffled his hair. "I'm sure you will."

CHAPTER 7

It was a muggy might, one of those weird ones that are neither light nor dark. On course to Sicily, in Mario's last voyage as a member of the crew, the Salonica was ripping through the calm, lead waters of the Adriatic to reach the Ionian Sea and the men, honouring the old tradition, gathered at the bridge.

Half sitting on stools and the rest on the floor with their backs resting against the wall, they were cracking and devouring the groundnuts they had bought in Durres, and, for some time, that was the only noise coming from the bridge.

Perched on the high stool by the helm, Mario had been turning the wheel with his feet, to keep his hands free and eat his groundnuts. Not long after, he'd started to get bored. He thought of telling them a joke to break the silence, but thought against it and got lost in his thoughts.

The developments had occurred with lightning speed, and, although he revelled in the unexpected and the opportunistic, he found himself not being able to evaluate everything that had been happening, especially concerning himself.

During their first voyage, Poseidon was on their side, and the calm weather lasted. Signorino had continued to send double speedboats, so they managed to dispatch the cargo easily, without any loss. Then, when they'd finished and had set sail for Albania, the weather got worse, and it took them double the time to reach their destination. By the end of the voyage, they felt exhausted, albeit in high spirits, knowing they would rest for the next couple of months.

The containers had arrived days earlier and had been waiting for them. The formalities were over quickly; they loaded the cigarettes and were off again in four days, happy to be departing from the misery of the Hodja and his unscrupulous ministers, who, supposedly by chance, had been passing by the port every day to say good morning and not to scrounge boxes of cigarettes, while their soldiers outside, guarding the port, drawn from hunger, would stick their starving mugs on the porthole, begging with their eyes for a cigarette or a plate of food.

Franco, who arrived on the second day by plane in Durres as Signorino's envoy, paid them for the previous voyage and arranged the details for the new. The next day he departed, delighted that he didn't have to travel with them, but equally impressed by Mario's progress in his language. Keeping the Italian book permanently in his pocket, Mario would never miss a chance to study whenever he had some spare time and, although the work was difficult, he stuck to his agreement his Charis, who had been categorical.

"Listen, Mario, if you want to tell me something, from now on you'll say it in Italian, otherwise I will not respond. Are you following me?"

He kicked the wheel softly to correct the ten degrees he'd missed, and looked at the men in front of him one by one, still eating their groundnuts in the dark, deep in their thoughts. Longing to end the silence that was bringing him down, he decided to liven them up.

Pretending to be absorbed in the compass in front of him, he stuck a peanut between his fingers and flung it at Phaedo's head, who was swearing at himself for his carelessness, as he'd swallowed a husk. The peanut hit him in the ear, and Phaedo looked menacingly at the Corfiot, but, distracted as he was, trying to release the husk from his throat, he didn't take it up.

Mario waited for a few seconds and prepared another one, aiming at the Corfiot this time. Laughing in advance for the fun that would ensue, he aimed and then suddenly froze.

The bright red light appearing out of nowhere in front of their bow was really intense and apparently quite near them. The glow that had suddenly washed the bridge turned everything red, forcing the sleepy men to start in panic.

"Hard astarboard…"

Charis screamed and rushed at the telegraph to ring STOP, while Mario was kicking the wheel like crazy to avoid the collision, but it was pointless now, as the light had suddenly disappeared and they were engulfed in darkness again.

Terrified, they all ran outside to light the spotlights, being quiet to pick up any noises, but there was nothing to neither see nor hear. The sea was calm and always devious, like she was making fun of them.

A very long fifteen minutes went by in utter silence, as they were searching with all the lights available to them. Later, they relaxed a little bit, started the engine, and kept looking, doing circles for an hour, but didn't notice anything out of the ordinary. They re-adjusted their course for Sicily, troubled, but livelier than before, in their usual setup, with Phaedo giving the finger to the Corfiot who was certain it was a UFO, Makis insisting that it was a submarine, and Burglas exorcising demons. Everyone disagreed with everyone else, except for the fact that it hadn't been a figment of their imagination. Later they seemed to have calmed down, but they did stay awake, watching, until it was dawn.

CHAPTER 8

The blonde at reception showed him discreetly around the corner. "He's looking for you."

An elegant bloke with a polite profile was reclining in the armchair comfortably, with a glass in front of him, and was reading his newspaper intently. "Who is he? Do you know him?" Mario asked.

The blondie fluttered her eyelashes flirtatiously.

"Should I?"

Mario preferred to play dumb.

"I don't know, my little girl. Maybe you should. Thanks, anyway."

He was in a rush to clear off the counter, before the blondie started the innuendos again. Lina was a nice person and up for anything; smart, energetic and pretty, but she wouldn't take no for an answer.

For a whole month, since he'd made himself comfortable at the small Pasalimani hotel, waiting for the speedboat to get ready, the blond receptionist had taken on all his errands, getting his documents and sorting out his contacts, so they had been spending a lot of time together. It wasn't enough for her, though.

When Mario explained to her that this couldn't progress any further—because he sees her as his little sister, he's into somebody else right now, he's terribly sorry, and other soppy things like that—the blondie listened to him carefully and nodded her little, golden head. As soon as she pierced him with those lovely blue eyes of hers, though, he knew this would be an arrangement that wouldn't last long.

From the direction he'd chosen to approach his table, it was impossible to see him. However, before he got there, the bloke noticed him, brushed the newspaper aside, and stood up, smiling.

"You must be Mario."

Mario interrupted him suspiciously. "If you say so..."

"You're exactly how they've described you. You can't fool me. Come, sit down. I'm John, well, Baffo, that's how everybody knows me."

He was smiling like a child and speaking so fast, you could hardly understand what he was going on about.

Dark, wiry, of average build, and young for the looming bald patch, with happy, vibrant eyes and cosmopolitan airs and graces, he still struck Mario as one of those odd types whom moustaches actually soften.

"Have you taken over the Salonica?"

"Yesterday morning at Preveza, and—"

"And Charis? How's Charis doing?"

"He's already departed for Italy to take over the other ship. He asked me to give you his regards and to remind you about what's written in your eyes. He said you'd know..."

Mario leaned back and, filled with his friend's image, who, for the entire previous month, had set himself to tutoring him in Italian, navigation, and meteorology, devoting all his spare time to Mario.

He'd taken it so seriously that he even sacrificed the five days they'd found themselves in Malta, when, half way into the week, the weather messed up their plans, and they had to run for cover to Valetta.

After a lot of pressure, the last evening, only after he was certain there wouldn't be another chance, did he agree to go out for totties, since the weather had calmed and they would have to leave the next morning.

Charis, who had more faith in Mario's abilities than Mario had of himself, gradually managed to infuse him with his optimism, teaching him to believe in himself; he struggled, he toiled, lost his sleep, but was vindicated in the end.

When they arrived in Preveza twenty days later, they had to part ways. Mario had grasped enough of the basics to feel more confident and, with a little effort, could communicate in Italian.

Signorino's telephone instructions left Charis at Preveza port, awaiting his replacement, and had Mario settling in a decent hotel in Piraeus, where he would be near the shipyard, pressing as hard as he could for the swift completion of the speedboat.

Mario caught up with his old mates, made some new ones, and was bingeing every night. At noon, though, he would go down to the shipyard without fail to inspect the boat, which had almost been completed. Signorino hadn't turned up to see it at all.

He raised his hand exasperated, leaning forward abruptly to cut off Baffo, who was still rambling on like a chatterbox. "Hang on. Have you seen Signorino?"

"What have I been saying? Are you deaf? He's sent me to meet you. Tomorrow he's coming as well; he'll stay with us until the boat is ready and then—"

"Slow down, Baffo. I'm really sorry, but I'm struggling to keep up with you. Can you not speak a little slower?"

"Yes, I know, it comes naturally. Other people have mentioned it, but what can I do? I'm almost forty, it's a little late to change now."

He repeated everything so quickly, almost unintelligibly, but, laughing heartily, Mario remembered Charis again, who'd warned him that it would be impossible to get mad at Moustachy. Gifted at winning his interlocutor over with incessant jokes, in about half an hour he'd made Mario relax and take to him, like they'd known each other for years.

They were even more elated when, later on, the receptionist, who'd been like a cat on hot bricks until her shift ended, settled herself down between them while they blissed out, and soon after, a gorgeous brunette joined them (Moustachy's date) proving that the ladies found him equally charming.

They proceeded with the requisite club hopping, as many as they could manage in one night, and when they got back to the hotel, wasted, Mario re-examined his views on platonic love and spent the night in blondie's room.

He found Baffo waiting in the lounge again and was really impressed that, besides a lock of hair that was facing the ceiling, outing his hurriedness, his mug was polished and rested.

"How do you manage, Baffo, to look as fresh as a moustached infant? Haven't we been boozing together all night? Why do I look like I've been beaten?"

Moustachy checked his watch, chuckling, and moved over. "It's almost eleven and Signorino said ten, otherwise I wouldn't have asked them to wake you up."

Mario caught his face in the mirror opposite and turned his head in disgust. "What the hell! The man is going to throw up when he sees me"

Still laughing, Baffo separated some notes, gestured at the waiter, and stuffed them in his palm.

"I know it's late for breakfast, but can you sort my mate out and also bring three black coffees together with that."

It was half-past eleven, and Mario was finishing his second coffee. Moustachy was wondering if Signorino had missed his flight and got up to ring him, when the revolving doors rotated, and Signorino appeared, following an energetic, bulky, middle-aged man.

Carrying a briefcase, upright, elegant, cool, and handsome like a Roman emperor, he walked a few steps, then stopped and looked around him.

He could easily make out Moustachy, who was waving from the back of the room, so he motioned the fatty ahead of him to follow, and they walked toward their table. Being closer, Mario stood up first to welcome them. Signorino hugged him, kissed him twice on both cheeks, and looked him in the eyes inquiringly. "Come vai, Mario?"

Mario saw the opportunity to demonstrate what Charis had taught him and returned the greetings in Italian, quickly and smilingly. An astonished Signorino hugged and kissed him again, very excited. "Bravo Mario! Bravissimo! Questo è un miracolo!"

Mario lowered his eyes modestly. "Thanks, but it's not a miracle. I've been tutored for three months…"

"But you've learned to speak in three months!"

"I haven't learned yet, but I am getting there…"

He was awarded five more bravos by the impressed Italian who was proud that he hadn't been mistaken in his choice. Afterward, they sat down, and he introduced them to the fatty he'd been dragging along.

"This here is Horacio."

The fatty heard his name and turned around to see what they wanted, sending a little kiss to the ladies at the next table.

"Horacio is our engineer, former head engineer for Alpha Romeo. He's an expert, as long as there aren't any women around when he's working, because he gets dizzy."

Horacio followed Signorino's gaze, who was eyeing the ladies, and burst out laughing.

"But, we're not working now…"

Mario studied carefully the laughing, curly-haired man with the round face and the ever-moving eyes and felt that he could count on him.

…

The taxi stopped at the gate of Preveza's port, about a hundred meters from the dock, but Mario didn't have the patience to wait by the security barrier. He got off in a rush, walked for the first few meters, and then ran to get there faster, while his heart was pounding irregularly from excitement.

Freshly painted ocean-blue, big and tall, the boat was rocking its bulk gently in the calm waters of the port like it was welcoming him. The Clara, its name drawn with calligraphy letters on the stern, brought back to memory Signorino's eldest daughter's huge black eyes, looking at him admiringly.

They'd stayed for ten days with Moustachy in Catania, in Signorino's house, much longer than required to pick the most convenient locations, for when they would be returning with the cargo. Young Clara always made sure she was with him, explaining things he didn't really need to know and constantly asking about Greece. Mario told her what she wanted to hear, and the slender girl listened to him, enchanted, while her enormous eyes were filled with admiration.

Inspired by the Greek history she'd been studying at school and living close to the ancient Greek theatre of Taormina, which was very popular during the summer, the young girl wanted to feel a little Greek and one afternoon, after surreptitiously downing a couple of martinis, she asked Mario if she really looked Greek.

In all seriousness, he told her that her beauty was reminiscent of their Goddess, Aphrodite. The young girl blushed, content, and replied that he was the spitting image of Apollo and rushed off, as she'd started to shake. Her infatuation flattered him, and he wanted to reciprocate. Her fifteen years and Signorino's faith in him, though, could not give room to any more frivolities.

His chance to offer her something as thanks came about two nights later, at dinner. As always, the whole family was sitting in a circle, and Nadia, Signorino's wife, with the girl that was helping her, kept bringing new dishes nonstop. The Chiantis were being emptied in a flash; Moustachy was telling Greek jokes to grandpa who liked them; and the youngest son, Dino, asked his father what the name of the boat was going to be.

That was something they hadn't considered and, initially, they looked at each other awkwardly, then laughed and started suggesting various names, each yelling to impose their own.

"Basta!"

Signorino banged his hand on the table, all the yelling ceased immediately, and he addressed Mario. "You're the coxswain. It's your choice."

"Are you sure?"

"Of course..."

Mario glanced at the young lady's gorgeous, laughing eyes across the table and raised his glass triumphantly.

"I shall name it Clara!"

The days went by pleasantly, in Moustachy and Mario's preferred pace, so any delays in the schedule didn't particularly bother them. Signorino, although apparently annoyed with the delays in the preparations, did let his hair down and relaxed his manners, and joined his best mates in whatever foolishness came to their heads.

For Mario it was a dream holiday, and he was thoroughly enjoying it, since, for the first time in his life, he could do whatever he fancied, without any guilt about overspending, because ever since they first went out Signorino had been paying for everything, true to his Sicilian masculine honour.

"If I notice anyone trying to pay the bill, our collaboration is automatically off. Capish?"

As early as the first day of their visit, they had determined the appropriate position to work at; they studied it carefully, checked it, and left. The next night, they went out at sea on a small inflatable boat, Mario measured the distances, chose a backup spot about two miles away, labelled them in his map, and their work was done. When they rang Horacio in Piraeus, though, to get an update on the boat, his answer marked the beginning of the delays to follow.

"Those devils, the Americans, haven't shipped the engines yet! They're saying the day after tomorrow again."

In Piraeus, eventually Signorino got fed up with the continued delays in the engines' arrival, especially since he'd paid for them in advance. He couldn't help it, though, as he wanted the special 270 horsepower ones and was forced to wait, for they were the pride of Mercury and the orders were multiple.

He got bored of waiting in about five days, left Horacio in charge, and, together with Moustachy and Mario, flew to Sicily, to choose the positions, making use of the wasted time.

They heard the same story from Horacio four more times, but, by that time they'd gotten used to it and didn't care that much. So when the engineer rang to announce that the engines had finally arrived and that the boat would be completed in a couple of days, Mario almost felt sad.

In their final nocturnal meeting, around the big drawing room table, everyone was present, including all the heads of various departments waiting for their instructions. Brusquely, yet in a friendly voice, Signorino briefed them, gave them directions, and asked if they had any questions.

For a business that had been started by their grandfathers, the lads rarely had any questions. It was routine for them, so they nodded, pleased that the period of inactivity had concluded, kissed everybody, and went off to organize their teams.

The comings and goings around the house calmed down and Mario attempted to read Clara's eyes, who looked unusually pale. The young girl was determined to keep her secrets, however, so she quietly lowered her eyes.

Signorino popped the champagne open, filled their glasses, and wished them Boca Lupo for good luck. Then he continued with his instructions to Moustachy, who would have to take the Salonica to Dubrovnik to load and return to the Ionian. There he would meet Mario in the new boat at sea, and tow him to position.

They arranged the details for a few minutes and then Clara, after her father's gesture, left the room, only to return immediately holding two little boxes with bows. Signorino kissed her proudly, and the colour returned to her cheeks.

Holding his daughter in his lap, the Italian deposited the little boxes in front of them and, smiling, attempted to make his voice sound formal.

"Can I have your attention, please? My dearest Clara would like to express her gratitude for naming of the boat after her and would like to ask you to accept this little present from her as a memento. Isn't that so, sweetheart?"

The young girl instantly turned poppy-red, and Mario removed from the little box the golden Dupont, which weighed his hand down, glittering. He raised it high, lit it, and thanked her with his best smile. The lighter's flame set Clara's huge, exultant eyes on fire, and Mario decided that this was a present worth keeping forever.

CHAPTER 9

The prolonged honking behind him jolted him out of his daze and obliterated the image of Clara's eyes, leaving only her name on the boat's stern.

"What's wrong, mate? You scared the life out of me. Why are you honking?"

"What should I have done, Mister? You've been staring at a boat in the dock for the past half hour. I've wasted enough of my day!"

Mario crumpled two tenners and flung them at the impatient cabby, like a stone.

"Go on, leave, I'll get back on foot."

His longing to get close to the boat had been gnawing at him ever since they'd boarded the flight from Sicily to Greece, so by the time they took the taxi from the airport, he couldn't wait any longer. He dumped Moustachy with the suitcases at the hotel and continued on to the port to see the boat right away, fully aware that, without keys, he could only admire it from the outside.

He returned to the hotel late, on foot, but cheerful, whispering songs all the way, so it didn't feel very far. Horacio had been waiting by the entrance, smiling, dangling the keys to the boat. "Have you been looking for these?"

Horacio, the engineer, turned out to be a real treasure, saving him a lot of hassle and confirming his initial impression, since all the time they were away in Sicily, he dealt with everything on his own. In the end, he moved the boat in a platform to the port, prepared it, washed it, and waited for Mario to hand it over to him. Mario hugged him.

"Mille grazie, fratello!"

The same evening at the bar by the port, the music was loud, the ladies were plentiful, and the youthful sweat mixed with perfume was filling the nostrils of the amorous Italian with desire. Clinging to the brunette he'd just met like a limpet, he was downing his fourth drink, flushed and hungry like a wolf, whispering in her ear. Strangely, she was constantly giggling and Mario was curious about how they communicated, since she couldn't speak Italian, and Horacio knew about ten Greek words all in all—only the dirty ones.

The brunette's friend was pretty, too, with a trendy long fringe covering her eye, she was sitting next to Mario, trying in vain to keep the conversation going.

Unperturbed by her efforts, Mario ordered another round of drinks and patted the engineer on the shoulder.

"Basta, enough, Horacio. Let's talk a little."

Careful not to distance himself too much from the young lady's sweet scent, Horacio half-heartedly turned his head and looked at him apologetically. "Ultima notte, Mario. I'm leaving tomorrow."

"That's what I want to speak to you about."

The engineer was a bit more interested, but still wouldn't disengage himself from the young woman.

"Tell me, Mario."

"Aren't you sad to be leaving behind all these girls?"

Horacio looked at the young brunette and sighed. "I'm very sorry Mario, but my work here is done and I have to go."

"But do you really want to leave?"

The Italian made sheep's eyes at the young woman and started losing his cool.

"Are you kidding me now? Of course not."

"Then stay."

Horacio slackened his grip on the brunette and gave Mario his full attention.

"How can that happen? I don't understand."

"I need you here with me for the trials. That makes sense, doesn't it?"

"It may well make sense, but Signorino will be expecting me."

"Don't worry about it. I'll ring him to say that I need you here, and he won't be waiting for you anymore. Agreed?"

"Are you sure, Mario?"

"Don't you want to stay? Leave it with me."

The engineer was so excited, he wavered momentarily about whom to kiss, but Mario pulled away in time and showed him the brunette, who was giggling again.

"You've pulled, but it wouldn't hurt to calm down a little. You've got a whole week ahead of you."

With a cigarette close to her half-open lips, the pretty lady to his left looked at him in anticipation.

"Have you got a light?"

The Dupont flashed and, for two seconds, Clara's eyes flickered in its flame.

"That's a very stylish lighter. Is it a gift?"

Finally Mario smiled and checked her out. "What did you say your name was?"

It took Moustachy only a day to get his gang together and the Salonica set off for the Adriatic to load, after they'd arranged with Mario their rendezvous after a week at sea. The boat's trials began the following day north of Lefkas, with a lot of theory and low speeds.

On the second Mario learned the basics about engines, could perform maneuvers at average speeds and kept congratulating himself on his brilliant idea to keep the engineer. Horacio wanted to return the favor for his wild nights with the young brunette, so he was determined to teach him in two days everything that he would have learned in a month.

On the third day, after the buoys, he motioned Mario to stop and stood beside him.

"Ready, Mario?"

"What for?"

Horacio grabbed the handles and propped himself up.

"Full speed, now. Go!"

"All the way?"

"Si!"

Mario took a deep breath and pushed the levers forward. The boat roared, lifted its bow high, then fell and darted like a bullet, while Mario pressed his back against his seat and felt his heart pumping.

As the minutes passed and the speed increased, the boat lost its touch with the water and the wash was leaving a waveless, white line. Mario's anxiety turned into thrill, and Horacio, laughing, signalled him to shut his gaping mouth, pointing at the redline on the dashboard and the speedometer at forty-five miles.

"Slow down."

Unwilling to give up his intoxication, Mario reduced the revs slightly, and the noise was reduced.

"Alora, Mario? What did you think? Fantastic, ha?"

"Why did you ask me to slow down?"

"I can't keep shouting. Stop, so I can explain."

Pulling a sour face, Mario pulled the levers back. The boat settled, turning the surrounding waters white with spume. Mario pulled out his cigarettes with shaky hands.

"Well, Mario. Tell me again; what did you think?"

Mario blew his cigarette smoke out heartily, moving his hands weirdly, unable to find words to express how he felt. "Are you going to tell me why you've asked me to stop?"

"Believe me, Mario, there will be plenty more opportunities for you to speed."

"Why not now?"

"Come and see."

He lifted the caps and showed him the steaming hot engines.

"High temperatures, Mario. Molto pericoloso! Capish?"

He explained that the manufacturer could not guarantee the safety of the engines working at maximum power for more than fifteen minutes, pinpointing that, with temperatures like these, anything could happen at any moment, and advising him not to give full throttle, unless absolutely necessary.

"Meaning?"

"Use it only if you're in danger of getting caught. Only then. But, of course, it wouldn't be easy to catch this boat."

"I wish that's the case, but why wouldn't they be able to?"

"Because the patrol boats reach no more than thirty miles, but, be careful, because if the sea is rough, or you're loaded, you'll lose plenty, too."

He told him that, luckily for them, La Spina, the famous patrol boat of the Finanza, the only one with maximum speed of forty miles that could threaten them, was permanently based in Bari and rarely ventured elsewhere. He also informed him that out of the two patrol boats based in Catania, the best gets to about thirty miles. If he happened to get shot at, he shouldn't worry about the boat exploding, because the petrol tank was covered with three layers of polyester. Even if he ever suffered any damage, he should never allow anyone else to touch the engines, until he got there.

"Where, Horacio, in the middle of the ocean?"

"All you have to do is tell me exactly where you are. I'll find you."

The rumour that one of the fastest boats in the Mediterranean was moored at the port spread around the small town quickly. Permanently present, among the curious bystanders watching their comings and goings, were the pretty blonde and the brunette who had been filling their nights. They used to wave their little hands proudly at the port, but they wouldn't dare get on board a second time. On their first and only ride, after about ten minutes, they were begging Mario, terrified, to return and when he finally brought them back, one of them was yellow and couldn't see, and the other was green, with an upset stomach. It took them about twenty hours to recover.

On their last date, Horacio let the girls move on ahead, stopping Mario at the bar's entrance.

"Domani we're leaving."

Mario looked at him, intrigued.

"Don't you think I know that?"

"Si, but a woman hasn't peed."

"What's happened, amigo? Are you so smitten you can't think straight?"

"Boca Lupo, Mario. For good luck. A female has to urinate onboard before it sets sail. It's a tradition."

"What?"

"Definitely."

"If that's the case…"

The girls were being difficult for about an hour, after initially flipping out at the eccentric request. They called the men perverted and kinky, then burst out laughing, followed them to the port, and peed on the bow, ill at ease. That's how the tradition was upheld, although the following day, due to set off, the boat still reeked.

It was a sunny Sunday, almost noon, perfect for the timewasters gathered to watch the departure. Although clearly worn out from his nocturnal adventures, Horacio couldn't bring himself to kiss the teary brunette goodbye. Mario, balancing his things on the boat, was quietly swearing at the right-wing grafter, who wouldn't sign the sailing papers before pocketing the hundred-dollar bill.

Considering it bad luck and an insult to his Greek honour, the pre-military dictatorship waste ruined his mood. Swearing the whole time, he started the engines to warm up, placed his cigarettes, lighter, and coffee thermos in the special compartment right of the dashboard, yelled at Horacio to get a move on after all his kissing, zipped up his tracksuit, and took his position in the control area.

The crowd moved closer together to get a better view, as Horacio was jumping in, releasing the rope. The pretty girl was blowing kisses, and Mario felt obliged to please them with a spectacle.

Having made sure Horacio had pitched himself, he pushed the levers forward. The crowd exclaimed when, with a deafening sound, the boat was raised commandingly in the air. Nobody, except for Mario, saw young Clara's present—the golden Dupont—sliding, bouncing, flying past his nose and plunging into the port's murky waters, darkening his soul.

CHAPTER 10

"Are we lost, Mario? For real?"

Drenched from seawater, the young Sicilian's long hair was stuck on his face, his teeth were chattering, and anxiety made his eyes glimmer strangely in the dark, yet he was trying in earnest to keep his voice steady.

Not having said a word for more than an hour, his mate of the same age rolled up on the bow, above the engine caps, to stay warm, and followed the conversation, shivering. "Is it true, Mario? Are we going to drown?"

Mario was also soaked to the bone and shaking, extremely tense, and the last thing he could tolerate at such a time was whining. Thinking he would need to hire a Greek assistant after this adventure was happily over, he pulled the young man from the lapels and pressed his face on his own. "Calma....calma. You seem in an awful hurry to die."

Energetic and smiling, the young men had boarded the boat early, making fun of the others left behind at the tucks, feeling lucky they'd escaped the daily routine, since, even for just one night, they would get the opportunity to taste adventure. Mario had sent someone to call Signorino, who came, worried. "Do you need anything, Mario?"

Mario showed him the young men, who, disregarding the necessary preparations for the voyage, were guffawing, teasing the men outside.

"Do you see? They are only coming just for fun."

"Is that a problem? Take others, if they're not suitable."

"It doesn't make any difference, Vincenzo. None of them are experienced at sea."

"Take more and pick the ones you want. They all want to travel with you, anyway."

No matter who he'd taken with him, he couldn't see a great improvement in his work. This was something he'd got used to by now, since in the past eight months he'd tried out most young men in the squadra. Sometimes, he'd single out a few and decide to keep them, but the rest, who hadn't travelled yet, felt hard done by and stood in the way. So, to be fair among them, they'd started drawing lots a little while back.

The young men who'd won that night could have never imagined Baffo the captain's irresponsibility, who fell asleep when he shouldn't have, resulting in their being lost at sea now.

Eager to always finish what he started promptly and efficiently, it didn't take Mario long to realize that it took them a long time to complete a trip, due to bad management and pointless maneuvers. He considered it carefully, then arranged with Moustachy to bring the ship to the position an hour earlier, and, taking advantage of the extra time, he was out, ready to load, two hours ahead of schedule. Signorino was curious.

"How come, Mario? Why so early?"

"To manage a second loading as well, Vincenzo. If you tell them to hurry up, I think I can make it."

That hadn't been done before, and he looked at him in disbelief, but, being a clever businessman, he didn't want to miss an opportunity.

"Do you think it can be done? No one has ever..."

"Yes, I'm telling you, it's doable."

Signorino didn't waste too much time pondering and gave his orders. The men surrounded the boat like locusts to empty it, Horacio refuelled and checked the engines quickly, so in about ten minutes, Mario was speeding off to sea again.

He located Baffo easily, who'd approached at twenty miles as planned, was reloaded swiftly and, a little after midnight, reached the shore again, amidst the squadra's cheering. Signorino hugged him, obviously moved. "Well done, Mario! You're the man!"

Ever since, when the weather was favourable, Mario would complete two voyages every night. Management and logistics were improved, cost and time were cut in half. Everyone was pleased with the way things had turned out, but they had to work longer hours, which was exhausting, especially for Baffo.

"Calling Baffo! Calling Baffo! Over!"

He released the switch and leaned forward to listen better. The night was filled with sounds from the annoying interference, which, mixed with the macabre wind whistling, exacerbated their precarious predicament. His agitation grew, and he felt his back unusually cold. He tried to convince himself that it wasn't fear that was freezing him, but the water dripping from the bulwark on his chest. He shook it with his palm to drain the water and attempted to contact Baffo, once again, without success.

The heavy wave splashing on Clara's side as soon as he'd left the microphone forced him to hang on to the wheel for fear of falling over and refilled the bulwark with water. Curled up like cats on top of the engines, the young Sicilians, a two-headed shadow, had been watching in silence. Mario took a sip and offered the bottle: "Would you like some?"

They shook their heads without speaking and Mario had to brace himself. "Listen, mates."

Their heads were raised slightly, showing they'd heard him, yet Mario persisted. "Can you hear me speaking?"

The Si, Mario sounded faint, but it was enough to prove that they hadn't fallen asleep.

"I'll only say it once, because it's impossible for me to watch over you all the time.

If you fall asleep, pneumonia will be the least you can expect to befall you. Comprende? Don't sleep and...start talking."

The young men stirred worriedly, and the voice heard was the one's who'd always ask the questions.

"Mario?"

"Yes?"

"Do you think we'll get away?"

"Get away from what?"

"Aren't we in danger, Mario? Be honest."

"I've been lost up to ten times so far. Have you ever heard of me being in danger?"

He was telling the truth that he'd been lost a couple of times, but none of them resembled this one, and he was fully aware of that. But the young men perked up a tad with what he'd said, and their fears subsided somehow.

The weather had looked dodgy since after noon, so he'd asked Moustachy to bring the ship even closer and save some more time. Although it would be dangerous for him, Moustachy readily accepted. Mario loaded and got the first cargo to the assigned position. He forced them again to speed up—to have enough time for the second—and was off in a flash to find Moustachy and reload. If the weather worsened, he would get a great opportunity to let off some steam for a few days, although he'd have to find a good excuse to avoid the guys from the squadra, who'd want to put him up. That way he could freely devote all his attention to the young girl he'd recently met. He was smiling, entertained by this prospect, enjoying the young men's enthusiasm, who'd been playfully relishing the speed, like contented tourists on a cruise ship.

The wind had picked up and the boat had been dancing on the waves, upsetting its guts, when the instrument panel indicated they'd reached their rendezvous. Mario slowed down and looked through the binoculars. He couldn't make out anything, but it was pitch dark, so he wasn't too concerned. Scanning the horizon, he continued forward for three more miles, put the engines on idling speed, and switched the radio telephone on.

Baffo did not respond. Mario sighed, lit a cigarette, and tried again. Swearing at Moustachy, he dropped the microphone and kicked the cabin door. The young Sicilians were startled.

"What's wrong, Mario?"

Mario raised his hands, obviously annoyed. "What's wrong?! Where's Baffo?"

The lads, who did not have an answer, kept staring at the sea, lost, saying nothing. Mario cracked his fingers angrily and stooped to check the pointers on the dashboard instruments.

"We can search for a little while longer, and then we'll see."

It had happened more than once that Moustachy would not switch the headlight on to assist him, as he considered it pointless and risky. Another time, he'd forgotten the radio telephone off, and, on a different occasion, he missed the position by ten miles without paying the slightest attention. Moustachy's carelessness frequently wore Mario out a tad, but he always managed to discover him within the hour, cursing him all the while, from the moment he reached the boat till he left again. Moustachy promised in earnest that he would be more careful next time, only to forget again the day after.

Relatively satisfied with the indications on the dashboard, he thought that he might have been too harsh on Moustachy (as it was highly likely he'd suffered serious damage or was too scared to approach their rendezvous spot for some reason) and decided to extend his search to a ten-mile radius. He wasted an hours' fuel and stopped again, about to explode with anger.

"Why have we stopped now, Mario?"

"I think we'd better head back. It's getting too risky."

The young men sprung up like they'd been stung by a dragonet fish.

"Go back without the cargo? How about the waiting squadra? Signorino will go mental!"

"I'll deal with Signorino, you imbeciles, and I couldn't give a toss about your squadra! I'm telling you, things are getting tight because we only have enough fuel for two hours, and, if we don't find them soon, we'll get stranded at sea while the weather is getting worse."

"Sure, Mario. You're the coxswain, you know best."

Mario sensed the ironic tone and got really cross. Despite his twenty-four years, he had been brought up at sea, part of a seafaring family, and it'd been ingrained in him from an early age that no one should mess with the sea. He swore at Moustachy out loud, had a little whiskey, and looked at them. "Would you rather we kept looking?"

"Of course, Mario."

"And you're not worried?"

"Why, is there a reason to be?"

When he brought the engines at idling speed again about an hour later, he informed them that they did not have enough fuel to return, and the young Sicilians' confidence went out the door when they feared the worst.

"What now, Mario?"

He showed them the cabin. "Make yourselves at home."

The young men looked at each other, confused.

"I don't understand..."

"The search is over. We're lost too, now. We'll move as slowly as possible to save fuel, and we'll request the position from the first ship we see."

"What if we don't come across any ships?"

"We'll see. There's no reason to fret about it now. It's better to get some rest."

The young man stretched his arms in despair. "Rest where, Mario? There're no beds in the cabin, just water."

"If you'd rather stay outside, stick by the engines to keep warm, and keep talking."

The young man just stared at him, without understanding. "Why Mario?"

"No particular reason; I just want to practice."

He seemed angry at them, but in reality he was mad at himself for allowing his temper to get the better of him and get into trouble, like a novice. Superstitious, without admitting so—like most seamen—he was certain that the sea would avenge their irreverence and that thought sent shivers down his spine. The minutes went by painfully slowly, and the waves grew bigger.

Mario was struggling to hold the boat in the channels so it could be easily navigated, but whenever it had to jump waves, fresh spume rushed in, soaking everything, while the cold was becoming unbearable. Right about then, the young men began whining.

He'd been calling Moustachy for about a quarter of an hour only to receive interference for an answer. His eyes stung from the salt, he was soaked from the freezing water, and to stretch his icy, numb legs, he was kicking on the cabin door, which frightened his assistants, but, crucially, kept them awake.

Daybreak was not much different from the receding night. It just got slightly lighter, enough for Mario to assess more clearly their dreadful predicament, the threatening sky, their isolation, and to start fuming when he realised that the tiny dot on their west was following a different route and was fading away.

He was draining the last drops of the bottle down his throat when he saw the ship. With very tense movements, he threw the bottle in the water, wiped the lenses on the binoculars using his fingers, and fixed them on his eyes. His heart pounded with joy when he realized that the ship's trajectory was convenient. He calculated that it was going to approach at around five miles, estimated he had enough fuel for a quarter of an hour, worked out his route quickly, and increased the boat's speed.

Accustomed to the lulling hum of the idling engine, the young men jumped up, filled with hope. "Mario?"

He directed him with his gaze toward the south. "A ship."

The young men hugged each other, rejoicing, and then rushed to kiss him, too, but he opened the cupboard in front of him and threw two lifejackets towards them. Their renewed terrified expression forced him to mellow.

"They're just for extra safety. We're not out of the woods yet, but it should be alright. Don't worry; we'll make it."

The young men sighed in relief, put on their life-jackets readily, and focused their attention on the ship ahead.

It was a Greek freighter en route to the Middle East, with its entire crew on the gunwales, watching suspiciously the strange speedboat approaching them. Mario aligned his boat with the ship's bridge, lee side, and stuck his head out of the cockpit. "What's the position, guys? I just need the position!"

Overcoming the initial shock, the crew lads, thrilled to have discovered a fellow Greek in the middle of nowhere, started messing around, and—convinced they could solve all life's mysteries at once—overwhelmed Mario with questions about every crazy story or legend they'd ever heard about.

Making a virtue out of necessity, Mario answered listlessly the first thing that came to his head, but the purposeless ordeal came to an end when the second mate re-emerged on the side.

The paper with the position landed on the Clara's deck wrapped around a screw. Mario picked it up, waved thank you at the second mate, and waited a minute for his assistants to catch the bottle of brandy the bosun had offered them. Then he switched his engines off as the ship got further and further away, leaving them alone again to be knocked about by the waves.

Fully aware that he could not afford to remain adrift for long, Mario quickly selected one of his ragged maps and spread it on the floor. The curious Sicilian—the one always asking the questions—was watching sadly the freighter drifting away and began saying something, but Mario cut him off. "Don't start again. At least now we know where we are, and, thankfully, we're not very far. We may not have enough petrol, but we'll get closer. That's better than nothing."

He covered a few miles with as much speed as the waves would allow, then stopped and called Baffo again. Like coming from another planet, Moustachy's voice, lost in interference, was barely audible. Mario was experienced enough to know he was on the right track, but it would be of no use persevering from that position, so he picked up speed again and kept going.

A few minutes later, he was staring at the petrol indicator, which was completely still and aslant. He wondered how on earth the engines were still working and called Moustachy again. He could be heard from afar again, but this more loudly and with less interference.

"Hello Mario! Mario, I can hear you, over!"

"Roger, Baffo, you wanker! I can hear you better now. Where have you been, you bastard? Give me your position. Over."

Like every time he was upset, Moustachy spoke faster than usual, and Mario did not understand a thing.

"Speak slowly, I do not read you. Slowly, do you hear? Slowly. Over!"

His second attempt was as incomprehensible as the first, and Mario was so furious, he was about to throw the microphone overboard, when he got the idea. "Baffo, I did not read you again. Say it in Italian this time, OK? Parla Italiano. Cambio."

The young Italians looked at him like he was not quite right in the head, but Baffo's Italian, reaching their ears, was crystal clear. Mario was marking everything down so distressed, that he wasn't quite sure whether crying or laughing would relieve his tension.

"I read you now, Moustachy. Alright, we're not very far. I should imagine I'll see you soon."

Shortly after, he caught sight of him and sighed. "I can see you now. Turn twenty degrees to the south, and I'm on my way."

He directed him so he could see him as well and smiled encouragingly at the youngsters, who had ceased celebrating ages ago.

"That was it, mates. Our problems are over."

He was lying again; only this time he didn't know it either. The left engine was the first to go, and the other followed suit.

They had been adrift for about an hour by the time Moustachy reached them, had been at risk of being overturned by the waves about ten times, the young men had turned blue with cold, and Mario, with a head like a wasp's nest, had been constantly counting his limbs, for fear he'd lost some.

After several attempts lasting more than half an hour, they finally managed to get on board the ship and left Clara being towed sixty meters away. His young assistants disappeared inside to get warm, and Mario headed for the bridge.

"Have you lost your mind, you wanker? Where have you been, you deplorable sod, I'll—"

"Come inside to get warm, or you'll get sick. Don't worry about such things now..."

"I've almost drowned twenty times over, and you're telling me to leave it now? You irresponsible wanker..."

Moustachy looked at him innocently. "I fell asleep, Mario. I'm so sorry, I was exhausted. Do you know what hell we've been through these past few hours? I swear to God, I thought you had drowned."

Such was Moustachy's disposition that words lost their meaning, and no conclusion could ever be reached. Mario knocked on wood to ward off bad luck, didn't say another word, and walked off. The half hour he spent in the hot shower curtailed his trembling, helped him recover his strength, and reminded him of his hunger.

It wasn't fatty Burglas's pretend bullying that forced the young Italians to get up and reluctantly abandon the warm, comforting safety of the cabin, but hunger. They systematically avoided Mario's eyes, ate hurriedly, and returned to the cabin to get some sleep and attempt to overcome the agony they'd been through.

Mario warmed his gut with a stew and headed upstairs for the bridge, composed by now, to discuss with Moustachy their next move. It didn't take them long to agree that it would be impossible to finish the job with this ship and to dismiss Makis's idea to approach the shore and make arrangements with Signorino, who would be extremely worried for sure.

They thought it foolish to risk even more for something that could be easily done the next day over the phone in the safety of Valetta's port. Even the five o'clock weather forecast confirmed that was a sensible course of action, since the unsettled conditions would continue for the next twelve hours. After the decision had been made, Moustachy turned to the Corfiot.

"What's our current course?"

"Three hundred and twenty degrees."

"Turn to two hundred and stay there until further precise instructions. We're off to Malta!"

As if Mother Nature wearied of finding anything interesting happening that day to illumine with her light, the day gave up and abruptly turned dark, enhancing the bellowing wind, which sounded even more menacing.

Being a strong craft, the Salonica stood up powerfully against the two heavy waves landing on its mask and proudly completed its tacking. Smiling cheekily, with his mind already savoring Malta's pleasures, the Corfiot released the wheel to return to its regular position, corrected his trajectory, and was just preparing to say something, when a sudden bang froze them. Before they knew what was happening, the second bang flickered the lights, and the third plunged them into silence and darkness.

"Right full rudder, Spyros. We've collided with something! Makis, get to the engine!"

Most of them, confused, rushed to the stern with flashlights to see what they'd hit, while the rest went down to the engine room to assess the damage, and Mario tried to make out his boat in the dark.

Tied up to the towing cable, the Clara was pitching relatively calmly in the waves and, at first sight, didn't seem to have any problems. Its distance from the ship, however, looked unnaturally short. Puzzled, he stumbled closer, and then he knew.

Guided by his screaming and careful to hold on to something so they wouldn't fall overboard, the panic-stricken men dashed to the stern. More courageous, Moustachy and Phaedo lay on their stomachs and suspended their bodies over the propeller.

The stern plunged like a lift severed from its rope and landed on the surface, making a terrible noise, then it suddenly flew off again, and, in the three seconds that the propeller was above water, the sailors could easily see the Gordian knot with the naturally created hawser, which, after getting coiled around the wings in the most bizarre way, stretched out to its limit, blocked the shaft and stopped the engine.

In effect, the propeller had been towing the boat and it was glaringly obvious that the taut nylon would not withstand the friction with the sharp blades forever. Apart from the blackout, the danger of losing the boat was imminent, and Mario was racking his brain to come up with some way of rescuing it, yet all of his ideas were countered by the waves. Moustachy got up and switched off his flashlight, grinding his teeth. "What's just happened to us out of nowhere? For fuck's sake! I'm going to explode..."

Phaedo pointed at the Corfiot, who was watching from behind, shivering. "It's that wanker's fault."

"Are you angry at me again, you idiot? Is it my fault that the cable got tangled in the propeller?"

"If you had gybed correctly, you knob, it wouldn't have slackened and gone under. But you lost your mind when you heard about Malta."

"Why don't you go fuck yourself, Phaedo, or I'll—"

Mario got in the middle to control Phaedo, who was moving threateningly. "Take it easy, Phaedo! He's not the only one to blame. It's everyone's fault for not being careful. Maybe it was stress, maybe exhaustion, or the weather. Either way, we all fucked up together."

Mario broke off the argument about liabilities, certain that it was nobody's mistake that had caused this, but the sea's vengeance, which he'd disrespected earlier, so he chose not to make a big deal out of it.

A little later, Makis managed to produce enough power to get some light with the spare engine, but he was pessimistic about the main and certain that the sudden blockage had jammed it for good. Specialized in emergency solutions and in on-the-spot inventions—like all Greek sailors—they were confident they would find a way out of this mess. They sat down, thought it out, and everyone had an idea to put forward, but none would hold up in this instance. The high waves were troubling the drifting ship; dozens of items were trailing back and forth, crashing and wreaking havoc. Nevertheless, they had hardly noticed the items, and no one bothered to pick them up.

Their assessment that the ship could take such weather and was in no danger of capsizing gave them a boost; they all thought, though, that the speedboat was a goner. The hornet's nest in Mario's head stirred again, and his eyes started to sting unbearably from the lack of sleep, but the thought of losing his boat drove him mad, and he decided to take action. He took his jacket off and began undoing his shoelaces hurriedly, but Baffo, who'd been watching him, realized what he was about to do, and started yelling. "What are you doing, you nutter? Are you preparing to dive?"

Mario replied with his head lowered, still undoing his laces. "I've got to get hold of the boat, somehow, Baffo. I can't just leave it to disappear in front of my eyes."

"Forget heroic gestures of this sort. Put on your clothes, and stop fucking around. You won't even get as deep as ten meters. What do you think fifty meters are like in such strong winds? Your local swimming pool? You'll drown before you can say Jack Robinson!"

"Alright, I'll wear a lifejacket."

'That's when you won't budge a meter. The wind will drag you away like a rubber tube, and we won't even find you! I'm telling you, forget it."

"I have to go, Baffo. It hurts my soul to see it like that…"

"Cut it out! You're not going anywhere! As long as you're on board this ship, I call the shots! Is that clear?"

They started contemplating again a solution to their problem, and time was passing by slowly, made even more miserable together with the night and the cold that was freezing their brains out. Moustachy got up like he'd suddenly remembered something, asked for an inspection lamp from Makis and for Phaedo's knife, got a rope ladder, and set about fastening it to the stern rails. Mario was baffled.

"What's going on, Baffo? Have you decided to commit suicide in my place?"

"I'll go down and cut the cable off."

"Are you completely out of your mind, Moustachy? You can't go down. It's impossible."

Without answering, Moustachy tied the inspection lamp, but the bow descended again right at that moment, sinking the lamp underwater, which burst with a bang. Baffo cursed the sea, switched the flashlight on, secured it between his teeth, and strode over the rails, preparing to go down. Lunging toward him, Mario barely grabbed his hand. Makis, who also rushed to help, grasped the other, and for a whole nerve-wracking minute they were struggling, groaning, to pull him up, while Moustachy was stubbornly resisting. It was only due to Phaedo's assistance, who lowered himself dangerously over the edge and caught him by the belt, that they managed to toss him back on board. Mario lay on his back on the wet iron floor to catch his breath.

"Why are you doing this to us, Moustachy? Aren't we tired enough already?"

"The propeller must be freed. I'll cut the fucking cable off."

"How, Baffo? By drowning yourself?"

"I can make it, you guys. It's no big deal."

"You really are completely stupid. If you'd gone down two more steps, you'd be history by now, and you're telling us it's nothing?"

From that moment on, Mario and the engineer kept a close eye on Baffo, in case he tried something stupid again.

They filled their stomachs with alcohol to stay warm and were chain smoking. They were all shaking like leaves in the winter wind, and it was almost three o'clock in the morning when Moustachy got up.

"Where are you off to, Moustachy? Have you got a date?"

"I'm going to bed. To hell with it!"

"Have you come unglued? We're adrift, and we're losing the boat any minute now. Besides, the way the weather is looking, we'll probably be cast ashore, and if we're not arrested, we'll get killed, and you, the captain, are heading off to bed? Have you completely lost it?"

Moustachy shrugged indifferently. "I don't give a fuck. If I don't get some sleep, I'll fall apart…"

He turned around and made for his cabin, while Mario was left staring at the door, trying to figure out the personality of this man, who, only a moment ago, was ready to sacrifice his life to save the ship, whereas now he couldn't give a damn about anything. Makis looked at him as if reading his mind.

"He's right, Mario. Go on and get some sleep yourself for an hour or so. You'll die on your feet, the way you're going."

"Sleep? How can I sleep?"

"You go, Mario. There's nothing we can do. The Corfiot will stay on the watch, as he's more rested."

Makis insisted a bit more until he was convinced, and Mario took off so that he wouldn't have to listen to him anymore. Dragging his feet like a convict, he got to the cabin where he usually slept, thrust himself on the bed in his clothes and shoes, and slipped into oblivion. He woke up suddenly, panting and soaked in sweat, looked briefly around him in confusion, sprung out of his bunk, opened the door, and almost banged his head on Baffo's, who was coming out of his cabin at the same speed. Without even exchanging glances, they turned together, like sleepwalkers, toward the exit and dashed to the bow. They simultaneously lay on their faces to examine the propeller, and then they jumped to their feet together, staring at each other, with nothing left to do but wait and see if the propeller would hold until daybreak.

The day was breaking, and the wind had abated, proving the weatherman wrong. The waves had subsided, and the Sicilian Mountains were rising imposingly above their heads, and Clara was floating peacefully in the morning dew, released from the propeller, beautiful and proud, like it was wishing them Good morning! Mario took a few deep breaths to control his agitation and be able to speak. "You'll probably think I'm crazy, but I dreamt about this, and..."

There was a strange glimmer in Baffo's eyes.

"What did you see?"

"I saw the Holy Mother! She brought me here to show me that the cable...had been undone. That the weather had calmed..."

Moustachy's hair, sparse though it was, rose in a chill.

"I've had the exact same dream..."

Mario, who would have never considered himself religious, got shivers down his spine.

"Baffo, this is a miracle!"

Moustachy approached the air intake, staggering as if intoxicated, and asked Makis to try the engine quickly; then, he turned toward Mario and pointed at the rocks ahead. "If the engine hasn't jammed, it will be a double miracle, otherwise we'll get smashed on the..."

The sound of the starting engine made him jump up and cry with excitement, putting new life into him. He ordered Makis to go full speed and, turning suddenly, he kicked the Corfiot, who was approaching them, rubbing his eyes.

"We would have gone down, you bastard, if we hadn't woken up while you were asleep on your shift. Get to the wheel now and keep one 180 degrees to get the hell out of here, and I'll see to you afterward, you bugger!"

The Corfiot ran limping to the bridge, thanking his luck for getting away with just a kick, and Moustachy, still tense, turned to Mario again. "Only one more, tiny miracle, Mario. We just need one more."

"What do you mean?"

"It's daylight now, and the helicopter will start patrolling soon. If we make it to international waters..."

Not even Mario could believe the confidence in his voice when he spoke: "We'll make it!"

That morning, the helicopter was nowhere to be seen. The young Sicilians woke up late in the afternoon, when everything had calmed down, without having perceived the slightest threat. Not that the others even thought of filling them in, though.

CHAPTER 11

Signorino lit his cigar slowly and ceremoniously, blowing out the smoke to the ceiling. "Well Mario? Will you manage?"

Although he asked him smiling, Mario knew that this time he couldn't avoid answering.

He'd asked him for the first time before dinner, and Mario slipped away, changing the subject. Signorino did not insist and was apparently bemused by Moustachy's endless jokes, but when the waiter cleared out the plates and brandy was served, he lit his cigar, reclined in his seat and cornered him.

"Well?"

Mario looked at him and sighed, crossing out his summer dream of ephemeral relationships and nonstop boozing on the Greek islands.

"Va bene, Vincenzo, I'll work."

Signorino's perfumed face lit up.

"Wise choice, Mario. You won't regret it. Besides, you've got three whole weeks ahead of you to rest as much as you want. We're starting in June."

Mario forced a smile and downed his brandy, trying to hide his discontentment. The unexpected summer voyages that had suddenly come about were not at all in his plans. They interfered with his schedule and his mentality, but he couldn't let Signorino down, who'd treated him like a brother. On top of that, he insisted that it was an amazing opportunity.

"Opportunity for what?"

"To work without danger."

"Are you taking the piss, Vincenzo? During the summer, when the patrol boats are plying the sea night and day? Isn't that why we stop in the summer?"

"Precisely; and that is why there's a higher demand. But we have our ways. And do you want to know something else? You'll be working in the light of day!"

Mario looked at him as if he were crazy.

"Daytime, with airplanes, helicopters, and patrol boats parading?"

Signorino was beginning to have fun. "Haven't I told you we've got our way?"

Mario looked at him in shock, but was fully aware that Signorino would never mess with business. "Go on, tell me more…"

"All in good time, Mario. And don't forget this is going to be your last trip with Clara. In the autumn, the new boat is going to be ready, unparalleled in the whole of the Mediterranean. Only this time, I'll name it."

"Really? How?"

Signorino smiled playfully. "Do you know what the lads in the squadra call you?"

"Oh. Mario Lafitte, I think."

"That's going to be its name!"

Mario felt flattered, and was intrigued; he forgot all about the girls and the islands and leaned forward to hear more. "Give me the details."

"In good time, don't rush it. What matters now is that you get some rest to be ready. You've had a difficult winter."

Signorino knew well how tough and exhausting the past winter had been. The bad weather that wouldn't let up, the incorrigible Moustachy with his crazy antics; the patrol boats that went after him plenty of times, and, on two occasions, the gunshots that made the boat's starboard side resemble a sieve. And as if that wasn't enough, right at their busiest time, NATO arranged to have exercises off the gulf, exactly on the areas they had been working.

The sky was polluted daily by the white patches left behind from the turbines of tens of Phantoms, which deafened you even in a multiple-mile radius. The sea was jam-packed with all sorts of war vessels moving in every direction, constantly confusing Mario, who didn't know how to cross and get to the shore without bumping into them.

Knowing he was being watched, for a few days he was circling around to bypass them and avoid an open confrontation, but he wasted his time and couldn't complete his runs. He finally got fed up and tried to pass through them.

The astonished American crew of the humungous aircraft carrier looked on as the audacious speedboat, like a tiny blue fly, swept past the immobile, iron mammoth. Then, as if they had been watching an entertainment show, they got excited and began throwing their little white hats in the air. Mario turned twenty degrees north of his course to conceal his true destination, dodged a destroyer, skirted around the exercise zone, corrected his trajectory, and got to his position to unload.

From the next day onward, every time he passed, all the crews on the warships were cheering, maybe because the boat's route annoyed their man in charge. The torpedo boat that approached intimidatingly to investigate them forced Mario to order his men to lift the tarpaulin from the cargo and show them that it was only cigarettes, so they could relax.

The torpedo boat moved away in disdain to continue its supposedly serious tasks, but a Phantom pilot thought it was a great opportunity to show off his skills. Making incredible noise, he descended almost vertically above them and just before he crashed their heads, he went up again, shaking their brains and upsetting every cell of their being.

They caught a glimpse of the reckless pilot, laughing away at the distress caused by his little game, and Mario's assistants responded to his laughter with internationally recognized gestures. The scene was repeated the next day with two other pilots, who weren't as daring. Immediately after, though, the Italian torpedo boat floating beside them went too far.

Its young captain yelled something through the loud-hailer; Mario's assistants answered back, annoyed, and a little later inveigled Mario to take up a speed race challenge.

The captain put a sailor in charge of starting the race with a small flag. For about two hundred meters, the vessels were neck and neck, but then the torpedo boat was left behind, losing the race. Mario's assistants were celebrating and jeering, so the captain of the torpedo boat, who did not appreciate being ridiculed in front of his crew, grassed up their route to the shore.

Led by the vengeful, informing young captain, the finanzieri ambushed the area and caught another squadra working the spot red-handed, confiscated two boats, a truck, a warehouse full of cigarettes, and imprisoned nine people for four years. Although Mario caused this misfortune unintentionally, he took it to heart, stopped working until NATO had completed its exercises, and returned to Piraeus to calm down.

Mario knew few things about Nick, the lanky young lad known to his peers as "the corpse," except that he was ugly, but very earnest, and that he'd worked as an assistant in another squadra's speedboat. But he hadn't met him before.

The hotel receptionist informed him that he'd been working for the Messina squadra, the one that had got into trouble, and that he'd narrowly escaped, but he'd made it back skint and had been begging to get work. When he first met him at the hotel bar, although it'd been five days, "the corpse" still couldn't stomach such an unexpected mishap in a position they'd been working quietly and uneventfully for two whole years. The lad was rightfully perplexed, but Mario, who could have easily enlightened him, did not really care for any additional turmoil in his mind. He pretended to have known nothing about it but started thinking that a good way to atone for his actions would be to hire him as his assistant.

The arrival of Nick's boss at the hotel changed his plans. Having run out of boats to continue his business after the disaster, the man had to find a vessel, but he couldn't, and, under the pressure of time and his squadra, rushed to buy an iron wreck. He left it in Corfu's port and went down to Piraeus to find a good coxswain to get it to Bari for him, to repair the broken engine and quickly get on with their work.

The money offered by Nick's squadra boss was not too bad for a few days' work, and Mario, who felt a tormenting secret obligation to help him, saw it as a great opportunity for Nick to finally become a coxswain in his own squadra and make a mint.

Mario came up with a thousand excuses to turn the proposition down and, egged on by the receptionist who was in the know, the bloke was convinced to give Nick a chance, who had been one of his own anyway. Besides, there weren't any other coxswains available, so the Italian, who was in a hurry, finally consented. As early as the same night, Nick, delighted for his divine fortune, flew to Corfu to attend the boat and meet the two young Africans, who would assist him in his passage.

Three days later, while Mario sitting at the bar, enjoying his first drink of the night accompanied by Lina, he heard the news on the television; the boat had sunk under terrible weather conditions close to Bari, and the bodies of two Africans had been found. Two days later, the news broadcaster announced that the sea had washed out "the corpse" as well, half-eaten by fish.

Two more weeks went by until Signorino notified him that the NATO exercises had ended, and Mario left for Sicily again, to collect Clara and get on with the half-finished cargo. He, however, had begun to change.

He hardly ever laughed anymore, and he frequently wanted to be left alone. He became edgy and threw himself into work. He was now more audacious than ever, albeit successful, so he performed better and thrilled the lads in the squadra.

Business was thriving, without any loss, quick and tidy, the lads were earning loads more money, which they felt they owed to Mario, as he was so good. They nicknamed him Lafitte because he reminded them of the pirate, and were extremely proud of him, often guarding him from danger.

The first cargo was done and, a month later, so was the second. Mario had been planning his holidays on a Greek island—to calm his nerves—but Signorino insisted that he and Moustachy would definitely have to stay for ten more days in Sicily, to humor the squadra lads, who wanted to show them their appreciation. But he wasn't telling the whole truth.

Moustachy looked at Signorino first, who was drinking his brandy, smiling, and then at Mario. "Just out of curiosity, Mario, what persuaded you? Because I didn't think you'd do it."

"Honestly, Moustachy, neither did I."

And they burst out laughing.

Certain they would have a good time wherever they were, Mario and Moustachy left themselves in the squadra lads' care, who put them up alternately, waiting for Signorino to arrange the summer cargo. That afternoon it had been Giovanni's turn. A bit eccentric and always stubbly, in his fifties, short, with white hair, tough, and dignified, Giovanni lived alone with his old aunt, who doted on him like a baby. The son of a landowner who was killed by a rival team during a major settling of accounts, he was Signorino's right-hand man, in charge of the members' discipline. He rarely said anything, maybe because he rarely needed to.

Mario had admired his style when they were searching for a position in deserted beaches and occasionally bumped into tourists or couples in cars, who were getting in their way. Giovanni approached them without speaking, looked at them, and lifted one finger to show them the way out of there. Without pointless questions or dangerous objections, the people nodded, packed their things hurriedly, and by the time he'd turned his back on them, they had started the ignition and disappeared, leaving the space free.

Inherited by his mobster father, the massive, derelict two-story building in the middle of nowhere, lost in a jungle of trees, bushes, and weeds, looked haunted. Without neighbours, and surrounded by a towering wall, a huge wrought-iron gate, and watchdogs barking at the slightest sound, it had been the perfect hiding place for those in the squadra who had to fade from view for a while, ever since his father's day. And Giovanni still upheld the tradition.

With one look, Giovanni kept the dogs growling at Moustachy at bay, and kissed his old aunt, who had been waiting by the door. Then he let Mario through first, and after they'd all gone in, he pointed at a chest on the left. He looked at him without understanding; the Sicilian smiled and lifted the lid. "Choose!"

The trunk full of guns disoriented Mario, and the laconic Sicilian repeated, "Pick one!"

Mario inspected a forty-five he recognized from his military service and looked at him. The Sicilian moved his head from side to side, searched a little, and placed a small automatic in his palm. "Astra, Spanish. Molto buono!"

With an imperceptible smile like a stamp on her weathered face, the black-clad old woman was serving them without saying a word, sliding inaudibly around them. The silence was unbearable, but Moustachy's attempt to tell a popular joke went to waste.

Mario took advantage of the stillness to determine what was in his delicious food, but up until he'd got full, he had failed to do so and wouldn't dare ask either.

The eerie silence of the haunted manor house had really begun to weigh on them, and when later in the afternoon Signorino went to pick them up as agreed, they welcomed him as eagerly as toddlers in a nursery at the end of the day, waiting for their caretaker to set them free!

In high spirits, Signorino announced that the business was settling and that he'd arranged the meeting for the following evening.

"What meeting?"

"You'll find out tomorrow, Mario. Tonight we're going to have fun."

"But that's what we do every night!"

"It'll be different this time."

The "admiral" in front of the impressive entrance crumpled his back hazardously, denoting his respect for Signorino, while he simultaneously managed to alert his manager, who hurried over, grinning from ear to ear.

Signorino seemed displeased at the lack of available tables, but the manager reassured him that he wouldn't have to worry about anything, ordered cocktails, excused himself for a minute, and disappeared in the distance.

The opulent, dimly lit hall smelled of sweet perfume and musky candles, the shapely silhouettes of the ladies captivated the men, the music was sensually soft, and the gorgeous blonde dancing alone, wearing only a g-string, electrified the senses.

The manager returned panting, but triumphantly. "Everything's ready!"

He stepped ahead to show them to the table, but after a few steps, the usual noises stopped. Mario was puzzled, but when he took a closer look, he noticed, to his surprise, the rest of the patrons rising from their seats. By the time they'd got to the middle of the hall, everyone was standing and applauding modestly, greeting them with smiles.

"What's happening now, Moustachy? Are they putting us on?"

Moustachy cracked up and pointed at Signorino, who was reciprocating the greetings, flashing smiles everywhere.

"Can you see how honoured our guy is? He's like a national hero!"

"A national hero! He's the chief mobster, Baffo! They must be pulling his leg."

"The man feeds a lot of people, Mario. He shells out money everywhere and puts himself at risk so that the poor can have cheap cigarettes. Do you get it? Even my grandma would adore him!"

Signorino raised his hands imposingly to stop the treating offers and sat next to Mario.

"Well, Mario, do you feel alright?"

"A little surprised, to be honest, but it's OK, I'm cool."

The Italian laughed.

"This is your night, so make sure you choose well."

"Choose what?"

"Look in front of you."

The ten breathtaking beauties lined up in front of their table were smiling, full of promise, in shades to cater to every taste. The nightclub manager leaned toward Signorino, enquiring with his eyes, but he pointed at Mario beside him.

"My coxswain, the Greek, gets to pick first."

Her golden hair was not much to his liking, her eyes, though, reminded him of the Aegean Sea he'd been longing for. And when she half-parted her cherry lips, he stopped mulling it over.

The manager smiled deliberately at him. "Do you speak Danish?"

"No, but I'm a fast learner."

...

The brand new Porsche was being tested on the crumbling, abandoned dirt road, but Signorino switched the lights on and stepped on the gas pedal. "It's getting dark, we're a little late."

Night had fallen for good when he stopped in the middle of nowhere, turned the engine off, listened carefully, and flashed the lights three times. From the opposite direction, the unseen car responded in the same way and left the lights on low. Signorino started the engine again and approached slowly, until their lights intersected on the road. He stopped the engine again, and they got out.

The middle-aged man emerged from the co-driver's seat and walked toward them, tall, upright, broad-shouldered, with an imperial stride. His horse-faced driver, fierce and skeletal, was following one step behind. The third member of their party stayed in the car, same as Giovanni.

They met where their lights had crossed, hugged and kissed without words. They lit the small cigars Signorino had offered them, and Mario spread out his map on the ground. The horse-faced man unfolded a similar one, took out a small felt-tip pen, and started copying the trajectories and positions Mario marked in his.

The fierce-looking driver asked a couple of things he couldn't understand and nodded. He finished in about five minutes, folded the map, and got up. Giovanni brought the packet from the car and gave it to Signorino; he in turn delivered it to the stout bloke, who passed it on to the horse-faced bloke. They kissed again, wished "Boca Lupo" and got in their cars to leave.

He woke up really late. The Sicilian noon in Catania was hot and stuffy, while the noise coming from the bustling square was unbearable. When Signorino suggested they had breakfast alfresco at the neighbourhood café, he felt like kissing him.

Mario set his mind tweaking the details of his upcoming trip and made himself comfortable on the wicker chair of the cool café to enjoy his cappuccino, while he gazed absentmindedly at the street.

The impressive dark Mercedes that stopped at the traffic lights in front of them merited everyone's attention, and the little flag with the curious insignia on the wing aroused his curiosity. He turned to ask Signorino, when he suddenly recognised the fierce, horse-faced driver on the wheel and tensed up in astonishment, but Signorino's kick on his shin brought him back.

Laden with stars and medals of honour, the chief in the back seat, erect and expressionless, resembled a statue. Only a couple of meters separated them, and it was impossible not to have noticed them. Yet up until the green light was illuminated and the armoured Mercedes moved forward, the chief remained immovable in his seat, without as much as blinking.

"What a bugger, Vincenzo!"

Signorino was staring at him, laughing, amazed at his surprise. "I know, Mario."

"Do you think he didn't see us, or is that the fib?"

"The fib, Mario. That's why you were kicked."

"Are you certain, though, that he's going to keep his part of the deal? In Greece, if you pay someone in advance, then they cut and run."

"I see, Mario, but this is Sicily, and we don't run. I promised you that you will work undeterred on this trip, and that's exactly what's going to happen."

"That sounds good, Vincenzo, don't get me wrong, but what happens if I run into a patrol boat? Will they also pretend they can't see me?"

Signorino burst out laughing.

"They'll see you, but they won't be able to come after you."

"Why?"

"Because the engineer, who's on the take, will sabotage their engine."

"What if it's a helicopter? Will they sabotage their engine and crash to their deaths?"

"They will never see you, because the pilot, who's in on it, only sees what's in his interests. Capish, Mario?"

Twenty five miles south of Sicily and obstructing the routes of those who were crossing the Mediterranean, the traffic from all kinds of vessels was relentless, except for the patrol boats, which were nowhere to be seen.

Polished by Horacio like new, the Clara was gliding softly under the hot sun, while the Salonica's crew were filling its gut with boxes of cigarettes, and Mario, in his swimming trunks, was sunbathing on the bow, waiting for them to finish. Invigorated by their working in daylight for the first time, Salonica's crew finished up swiftly.

Mario set off for the shore, enjoying the speed on the calm waters as if he were on a recreational trip. He played with the wind to keep cool, entertained himself like a child performing maneuvers, and a few miles before he arrived, he stopped to check the position he was passing through for the first time. He looked around, humming a song; then he extended his neck, dropped the singing, and grabbed the microphone without removing the binoculars from his eyes.

"Calling Vincenzo! Calling Vincenzo, quickly! Over!"

Signorino delayed, and when he answered he sounded out of breath.

"Come in, Mario. I saw you stopping. Have you got any damage? Should I send Horacio? Over."

"We were mistaken, Vincenzo. Do you know where this course is taking us?"

"To the beach, as you're coming, Mario. We're waiting for you here. Isn't that what we've said?"

"Agreed, but you forgot to mention that the beach is going to be packed with two thousand people swimming. Are you out of your minds? Someone is going to get killed!"

"Is that why you've stopped?"

"Of course! It's chock-full. You can't even slide a canoe through."

"But the people will move out of the way, Mario."

"What do you mean?"

"Leave it to me, Mario. You approach normally, like you do."

Even more confused than before, he set off in low speed. Then he figured he had nothing to lose and pushed the levers forward. The boat rushed inland with all its might, roaring like an airplane. The shore was fast approaching and he was about to slow down again when the people on the beach, alerted by the noise, turned their gaze toward the sea and saw him. Their reaction was immediate, impressive, and had nothing to envy from veterans in readiness drills.

Starting from the open sea, the crowd opened up toward the beach like a curtain. Parents, umbrellas, children, and buckets disappeared in the blink of an eye, letting the fresh sand glitter like gold from the seashore to the road, where the trucks had already begun the approaching maneuvers. Under the eyes of hundreds of spectators who abandoned their swimming to watch the operation, Mario switched the engines off and stuck his bow in the sand.

The truck approached in reverse, the lads formed their chain and started unloading, and Mario, pulling bewildered faces, jumped out to meet Signorino and Giovanni, who were coming toward him, smiling.

"Didn't I tell you they would leave? Trust me."

"Sure, alright, but loads of people, Vincenzo. Far too many. Do you get me?"

"Meaning?"

"There'll always be squealers among such a huge crowd, won't there? If someone makes a call, we're in trouble!"

"Oh, no, Mario. That's impossible."

"Really? How so?"

Giovanni mumbled something to Signorino.

"Can I tell him why?"

"Go ahead."

"Because, believe me, Mario, none of them want to sport artificial legs."

Giovanni had never been more extravagant with words, and Mario appreciated it. With a baffled expression still on his face, but much calmer, he left again in a rush for the open sea to reload, while observing behind him he could see the gap waning.

When he returned three hours later, the crowd had thinned out considerably, and on the third trip, at dusk, there was hardly a soul left to care.

The daily trips to the beach continued in the middle of the summer quiet and undisturbed, without informers, just like philosophical Giovanni had predicted. They had almost completed the cargo when one day the helicopter springing on them all of a sudden agitated them, but it continued on its course without any interest. The following day, the patrol boat spotted them again and moved swiftly against them, but a little later it disappeared, proving Signorino right once more.

When the cargo had been finished off, Mario, moved, handed the Clara back to Signorino. Mario was as dark as coal, with his pockets full of money, in high spirits and he found Moustachy's proposition to continue their sunbathing in Malta hard to resist.

He took the Mario Lafitte over two months later, in early autumn. The new boat was ten feet longer, with bigger, state-of-the-art engines, more capacity, and seven miles per hour faster than the Clara, so it quickly became notorious.

Mario was clearing his cargos in Catania easily, relishing the patrol boats' hopeless chase, so, hooked on the boat's amazing abilities, he had no objections to Signorino's new proposition to assist the Naxos, the squadra's other ship, working in Napoli.

He was disappointed not to meet his friend, Charis, who in the meantime had been replaced by another captain unknown by Mario, but only when the time came for the first trip did Mario realize what Signorino had meant when he talked about helping out. He found the Naxos awaiting in its position, outside of Capri, loaded and preparing to depart, when the captain stopped him. "Why are you leaving, Mario?"

"Why am I leaving? What sort of question is that?"

The captain looked uneasy.

"Hasn't Vincenzo explained it to you?"

"OK, you explain it to me."

"You'll go when the others load, too."

"Which others? Are there more?"

"They'll be here soon. You got here early."

"Hang on, because I don't quite understand. If you have boats, why did you drag me all the way from Catania?"

The captain pursed his lips, preferring not to answer, and then Mario knew and sighed.

"You brought me over here to be the bait, like a hare to be hunted by the patrol boats? You bastards?"

"Take it easy, Mario. We didn't bring you. It was Signorino's idea."

The trouble for the Neapolitan coxswains had begun two months earlier, when customs employed a third boat in their pursuit. The new patrol boat could reach speeds of up to thirty-five mph, would not balk in bad weather because it was bigger, and, assisted by the other two, had one success after the other. The contraband teams were losing a ship with its cargo per week and were starting to tear their hair out, but the problem would not let up. That's why they were forced to suspend their activities until they'd decided how to react.

In a meeting with the other squadras of the area, Signorino was clear that if they didn't put their differences aside, they would all go hungry in the months to come. When he suggested common cargos with all the vessels together, travelling in one group, they looked at him in disbelief. As soon as he added that he would run the show and that he would bring the bait, they immediately agreed.

Eight more boats arrived from various directions within the next hour and loaded from the Naxos; then they approached Mario to make the final arrangements, and it was dark by the time they all set off for the shore.

In an arrow formation and average speed of thirty miles, the nine black ghosts were slashing the dark sea with nine white lines and among them, and somewhere in the middle, Mario, poised to be the sacrifice, was drawing up his plans to fool the beasts and save the herd.

They moved on to the gulf of Napoli without any incidents, leaving behind them the dark mass of Capri, and Mario had started to relax, when suddenly the patrol boats doubled the tall reefs and surged toward them with all the speed at their disposal.

Trying to confine them in their beam, the huge headlights were scanning the darkness, while their sirens were shrieking, and in the pandemonium of so many noises, the gunshots lost their resonance and sounded like they came from children's toys.

While the man with the loud hailer was screaming hysterically, ordering them to stop, the coxswains revved up their engines to the max, and, following the plan, they started overtaking Mario, leaving him alone.

Fanning out to conceal their destination, the vessels were drifting away from Mario, and the big patrol boat approaching could not help but take the bait. True to the belief that the weakest prey is the easiest to capture, the patrol boats set sail to circle and devour him.

Mario maneuvered supposedly indecisively, allowed them to get even closer and then revved up slightly, steadying a safe distance from the bullets. He continued the pretend desperate maneuvers, headed across to Ischia, lead his pursuers away, in the opposite direction from the rest of the boats, which had reached the position undeterred by then.

Mario put up with this game for ten more minutes, then getting close to Ischia, he pretended he was making for the open sea again, suddenly bolted toward the bay, gained full speed, went past the old patrol boat, which didn't even have time to see him, and disappeared into the veil of darkness. Five miles further down, he corrected his trajectory and headed for the position.

...

"That trick won't last forever, Vincenzo. As soon as they get wind it's the same lure, it's a done deal, and you know it."

"You're right. I know. Just one more trip with all the boats to collect the rest of the cargo, and then we'll resolve the problem"

"How, Vincenzo? We'll face the same difficulties in the next cargo."

Signorino grinned with a certain look, all too familiar to Mario by now. "I told you it's going to be settled. Don't you believe me?"

As soon as they loaded the cargo the following night, Mario asked the coxswains to form a circle around him as they clarified the swindle and checked their radiotelephones. He left them there, setting off first on his own, at an average speed. A few miles before Capri, he stopped the boat to light a cigarette, checking on the happenings in the bay through the binoculars.

He made out the foremost light of the new patrol boat, which lurked behind the reefs. He wished he could convince them he was in trouble so that they'd go after him and set off again with average speed, on course toward them. He drew closer than half a mile, but the patrol boat wouldn't move, and Mario started devising new ways of making them pursue him, mocking their incompetence. Just before he'd overtaken them, he saw the spume on their bow and sighed with relief.

His average speed allowed them to get nearer quickly and their attack did not have the commotion of the night before. Deeming their siren an unnecessary hassle, they only lit the headlight and screaming at him from the megaphone, ordering him to stop, which could be heard loud and clear. Playing the idiot who'd just noticed them, Mario turned his bow toward the open sea and revved up. The patrol boat followed him full on; Mario let them edge him even more and turned for Ischia. The hysteric bloke got really cross, started the siren, and fired a shot to scare him, but his screeching became unintelligible, and Mario unhooked the microphone, laughing, and alerted the coxswains that the road was clear and they could set sail.

He let the shrieking captain think he was within his grasp if they continued on to Ischia, since the rest of them had been lurking there to corner him. He consulted his watch and turned slightly toward the open sea. The aged patrol boats popped up noisily to block his way; Mario performed some clumsy maneuvers on purpose and dragged them out to sea.

For a few more minutes he kept on pretending until the patrol boats tried again to circle him. He decided he'd had enough and spun suddenly toward them and shot past them, leaving his pursuers in shock, staring in a daze at the white trail he'd left behind.

The cargo was distributed on the market without any trouble and the squadras picked up again. Mario Lafitte soon became known in Napoli and the most wanted boat in Italy. Laden with laurels, Mario didn't feel like resting in Greece because of the dictatorship, readily accepted his new friends' invitation, who bent over backwards to thank him.

On the eve of his departure for Sicily, Signorino cornered him once more.

"He's a friend, Mario, and I'm indebted to him. Besides, Palermo is on your way. I'll notify them to be expecting you. Alright?"

"I don't want to be the lure anymore, Vincenzo. Do you know how exhausting it is? Not to mention that I sweat blood for other people to make a mint."

"On my honor, Mario, I've made it clear to him. One last trip and you're off to Catania. That way I'll return the favor. Agreed?"

"I'll go, Vincenzo. It's not a problem, as long as it doesn't become a habit. Who's going to continue the job here, though? Have you found someone else?"

Signorino winked at him. "We'll manage, don't worry."

At the break of dawn on the following day, just before he set sail, the youngster guarding the boat informed him that the new Finanza patrol boat had suddenly burst into flames during the night at the port and was completely destroyed...inexplicably.

CHAPTER 12

The information that La Spina, the jewel of the Finanza's patrol boats, had set sail from Bari to the South was passed on promptly from their people there, but they didn't pay much attention and completely forgot about it in just a few days.

Mario had returned to the old haunts of Catania for the past two months, feeling right at home, and the work continued in its familiar pattern, bordering on routine. Relying on his boat's great abilities, the perennially impatient Mario became even more audacious and started travelling through heavy storms or under the noses of the wrecked patrol boats, which avoided going after him pointlessly and instead concentrated on safer targets.

"The barometer keeps going down. Don't complain later that I haven't warned you. Just to be clear."

"I'll bear that in mind, Moustachy. You make sure you don't fall asleep and make me look for you again."

"It's going to get worse."

"Alright, alright. Mind your own business."

He'd also been watching the barometer for the whole day and the idea that he'd have to travel in a strong wind did not thrill him, but neither did it particularly worry him, since he knew that even if his speed was reduced as much as twenty miles, he'd still be faster than the wrecks pursuing him.

He was given a hard time by the waves, soaked part of the cargo that had been exposed, and took double the time to arrive. As soon as he'd unloaded, though, he made his mind up.

"I'll go again!"

Signorino raised his hand to stop the men who were leading the boat to the shed to hide it.

"Are you sure, Mario? It's awfully windy today. Perhaps it would be better if you stayed here."

"I think I might go, Vincenzo. Besides, the patrol boats hardly venture out of the port in such weather."

"That's right. OK."

He drove hastily until he'd burst out of the bay, then was forced to slow down and turn a little to the right to avoid getting all the weather directly on the bow. He checked the time and devoted his attention to the tumbling compass. Later into the night, the wind started picking up. The waves were getting higher, and the sporadic flashes of lightning tearing through the darkness were illuminating the effervescing crests, creating the illusion of mysterious angelic shapes that one minute looked at him solemnly and disappeared the next. His mind wandered wildly, but he kept pulling himself back to reality and the compass. The next lightning bolt struck close to him, jolted him into fright, and transformed its usual illuminated scene, replacing the solemn figures with a huge patrol boat coming at him in high speed.

Mario closed his eyes and shook his head to disperse the illusion. When he opened them again, though, the patrol boat was even closer, and, albeit it was sailing in complete darkness, he didn't need another lightning strike to make it out. Reacting through instinct, as his mind was out of sync, he positioned his bow on the first available passage and pushed the levers forward with all his entire body weight.

Being weather side now and fretting about the bow hitting a wave and cutting him off, he zigzagged constantly through the waves, pleading out loud with his engines to pull through, freezing with terror every time the propeller got out of the water, catapulting the pointers over the limits.

Concentrating on the waves and disregarding his blind course, he was struggling to keep the boat in channels he could speed in and was stealing glances at the patrol boat behind him, which, having failed to catch him off guard as planned, switched on its lights and was pursuing him openly now, with the confidence of a cat cornering a mouse. Certain for panic-stricken prey that was running beyond hope, the large patrol boat sank its bow in the water, only to re-emerge terrifying and more menacing, keeping its distance, indifferent to the storm, and with time on its side.

Soaked through the bone, but dry of ideas and determined to fight till the end, Mario was racing, trapped in a course without direction, groaning from the knocks and talking to himself, awaiting at any moment the damage that would stop him. The distance became dangerously shorter and he knew they would reach him in a matter of minutes. Mario turned to his front in desperation; suddenly he stretched out, looked closer, and his heart pounded.

The tall mountain was unfamiliar, but seemed like a gift from heaven in the midst of his desperate course. Screaming with tension, he kept zigzagging to maintain his margin, reached the cape, tilted to the right, and found himself in calm waters. The distance started growing sharply, and Mario, with a nervous laughter, showed them his fist. Then, slightly calmer, he checked his dashboard and glanced behind him yet again. The patrol boat that was once charging after him was stopped now, which baffled him, but he assumed it gave up the chase because it couldn't reach such great speed. Grimacing ironically, he turned to his front once more precisely when a rock was passing by him rapidly, like an optical illusion.

Before he had time to fathom what he'd seen, a second, even bigger rock scraped past and chilled him to the bone. He then knew why the patrol boat hadn't followed him, and after looking more closely and realizing the mess he was in, his chill transformed into a continuous shudder. Crazed with anxiety, he dodged a low one at the last minute, almost crashed on a taller one further down, and he pulled the levers to stop the boat just ahead of a rock cluster that walled his passage.

Breathing heavily like he'd been sprinting, he looked around, still unable to believe his luck, and began steering the boat out of that hellish area, very slowly and carefully, while the patrol boat was nowhere to be seen.

It was almost daybreak when, with his stomach tied in a knot and his knees still trembling, he arrived at his post. With the astonishment and the yearning of someone who had just seen a beloved dead relative coming back to life,

Giovanni—the only one there—embraced him, his black eyes welling up, heavy with regret. "I'm sorry, Mario, my brother, but we didn't have enough time."

Mario tore himself away and looked at him. "What for, Giovanni?"

Ashamed, the tough Sicilian lowered his eyes. "You had already left, when we found out that it had come to Catania to pursue you."

Mario knew the answer before he'd even asked. "Who was it, Giovanni?"

The dejected Sicilian lowered his head. "La Spina, Mario."

It was late in the afternoon when he opened his eyes, grateful to beautiful Clara for waking him up, delivering him from the nightmares. He found almost all of them together in the living room watching television intently, and Signorino beckoned him to sit near. "Listen to him, Mario!"

The bloke on the telly looked savvy, had a celebrity air about him, and was wearing a white uniform. He was speaking with a placid assertiveness and was explaining to the reporter that it had, indeed, been the first time that a smuggler had escaped him, but this had only happened because the coxswain was extremely competent and definitely local, as he knew the reef area like the back of his hand. He went on to promise that the La Spina would not leave Catania until its mission had been accomplished, namely to arrest the coxswain and deliver the speedboat to the authorities.

The patrol boat's captain added more along the same pompous lines and when the reporter asked him what, in his opinion, the contraband boat had been transporting, the smirking beefcake pulled a mysterious face and stated, "For the coxswain to be have risked so much, I'm certain it must have been something of great value."

The arrogant captain finished the interview promising once more that the next time he would speak, he would be towing the contraband boat to the port. The gang burst out laughing, making fun of him, and then Signorino put his hand on Mario's back and looked at him solemnly.

"Promise me."

"I don't understand."

"Promise me that Mario Lafitte will never fall into their hands."

"I have no intention of getting caught, Vincenzo, if that's what you mean."

"I'm talking about the boat. If you're ever in danger, founder it to get to the bottom, because if they get it, we're lost!"

"Why?"

"Because Mario Lafitte is a great catch for them, Mario. They'll turn it into a patrol boat, and none of us will escape. Then we'll have to kill ourselves. This boat belongs to us. Capish? That's why you must promise me."

"They're not going to take it, Vincenzo. I promise."

On the same evening they planted their watch at the port to keep them up-to-date with the patrol boat's movements. They let a few days pass by and notified Moustachy to return from Malta, where they'd sent him to lie low until things cooled off. The news about the failure of the terror of speedboats to catch the Mario Lafitte dispersed the myth of the invincible patrol boat and was quickly spread throughout Sicily, boosting the morale of contraband crews. At the same time, the name of the vessel that had escaped the patrol boat became a legend and its coxswain the most sought-after.

Three evenings later, Mario alerted the squadra to get ready, made sure that the La Spina remained docked, and set off carefully to meet the Salonica and collect the cargo.

On his way back, just before he'd entered the bay, he slowed down and—almost completely silently—slid by the port and reached his post. The business took off again, but with only a single trip per night, since there wasn't enough time for the second; their nightmare, the La Spina, apart from two or three patrols during the day, had not budged during the night.

The pleasant news arrived in the afternoon by the young lad responsible for monitoring the port traffic.

"It's gone, I'm telling you. It has departed!"

"Are you sure, Marco? Maybe it's still on its round."

"For ten hours? It's never taken longer than four."

"Did you see which way it went?"

"I thought it was to the north."

"Then it's probably on its way back to its base in Bari, but it's far from certain. What do you think, Vincenzo?"

Signorino was ecstatic.

"He's gone, Mario, the bugger, and empty-handed at that."

"Maybe it's just a decoy. It's better to wait until we get word from Bari that it's arrived there."

"Nonsense; he's seen that there's nothing he can do and left to avoid further embarrassment. We can wait for a few more hours to make sure, but why waste the night?"

Mario couldn't quite swallow that, but was ashamed to show his trepidation, so he agreed, shrugging. "You're the capo."

He gave Horacio time to adjust the engines at his lei-
sure, picked two of the best lads to assist him, stalled as
much as he could, and eventually, when it was past ten
o'clock, after Signorino had started giving him funny looks,
he reluctantly decided to set sail, with doubt weighing on
his shoulders.

Observing everything that seemed suspicious, he
crossed the bay's tranquil waters cautiously, passed the
cape, and reached the open sea without any problems while
his apprehension, however, did not subside. Rear-guard of
the latest southerly wind, the swell was heavy and slightly
obstructing his way, but the night was pleasant and calm,
with a murkiness that rendered it ideal for their work. A
skilled captain, Bafo performed the appropriate moves and,
despite the heavy waves, managed to throw five hundred
boxes onboard the Mario Lafitte without losing a single one.

Before heading back to the shore, he scanned the horizon meticulously without seeing anything suspicious. He,
then, repeated this two more times on the way back, yet
his uneasiness wouldn't let up. Looking constantly around
him, he reached the bay's tranquillity, cut a touch across,
and let the boat glide through the dark waters.

As he was got closer to the post, his anxiety started
to settle little by little, and once he communicated with
the others outside and Giovanni reassured him that everything was clear, he completely relaxed and cursed himself
and his stupid instinct, which was making a fool of him.

Almost two miles before he arrived, fuming at his fears
that had taken the better of him, costing precious hours,
he checked his watch to estimate if he'd have enough time
for a second trip, hoping to make up for lost time, but his

assistant's outstretched hand pointing at the red light flashing in the sky above the port messed up his plans.

"Mario, a helicopter!"

Before he'd had time to look through his binoculars, Giovanni's voice on the radiotelephone sounded worried.

"Mario, I've just been warned that the wrecks are getting ready to leave the port."

Mario muttered a few expletives, saying goodbye to the second trip he'd been planning.

"Alright, Giovanni, don't worry. We'll have enough time to unload. They'll take a while to get here."

"How about the helicopter?"

"It won't be able to locate us without backwash, and I'm coming in slowly. Where's Vincenzo?"

"He's waiting for you outside, in Etna."

He controlled the boat so it could float freely with the engines on, and while the squadra lads began unloading, he grabbed the binoculars again and looked curiously at the helicopter flying around the bay and at the old patrol boats, which were sailing on a steady course directly to them. Giovanni went near him and looked at the sea as well. "Can you make any sense, Mario? The buggers are coming straight here."

Mario frowned, released the binoculars, and lit a cigarette.

"What seems odd is that they're going all-out to get here, even though they know they can't catch me."

"They seem to know where they're going, Mario. Why is the helicopter still there, though?"

Giovanni's question was valid; Mario looked at the helicopter pensively, and all of a sudden the bells that had been quietly ringing in his mind finally sounded the alarm. "It's waiting for me, Giovanni! We've been set up. Hurry up!"

The Sicilian rushed to urge his men to speed up. Mario clutched the binoculars and climbed on his seat to get a better view. At first quick glance on the gloomy horizon, he couldn't see anything. But afterward, when he looked more closely, he saw it, and it was like he'd been punched in the face. Dark, at one with the night, the massive patrol boat could have crashed their heads before they'd even seen it if it hadn't been for the frothy moustache around its bow, which betrayed its speed.

Screaming at the men to drop everything as it was, Mario jumped on the cockpit and turned the boat around immediately, taking with him three men that didn't have time to jump off the boat onto the dock. As the patrol boat was approaching at around two hundred meters, he swerved to the opposite direction and went at full pelt. With ideal ballast the weight of the cargo they hadn't managed to unload, as well as the men that had been trapped on board, he rapidly reached full speed and increased his distance from La Spina. This way, however, he was racing directly at the other two patrol boats, which were approaching, intending to cut him off, while the red light in the sky stopped drifting and flashed more brightly. Speeding with open maneuvers to obscure his intentions, he became equidistant from all of them and was devising his next move when—as a demonstration of their advanced training—the patrol boats and the helicopter switched on their headlights and yelled at him to stop, firing a burst of warning shots.

Flashing past, Mario performed a semicircle, moved behind the old patrol boats that were slow to react, accelerated for another half a mile, and abruptly came to a halt. He turned to the right and moved silently away in low revs, far from his residual spume, which was guiding the helicopter. A little further down he stopped, covered the glistening dashboard with a towel and waited.

The helicopter reached the end of the white trail it had been following, hovered about for a while until its next move had been decided and kept searching slowly and methodically with its headlight in all directions. Mario moved gently, in the opposite direction from the light beam and paused again. Twice the helicopter flew past without spotting him and continued its hunt further down. Someone from the closer wrecked patrol boat saw him, though, and started screaming and shooting, forcing Mario to speed up again to escape La Spina, which was fast on its way.

He ran like mad for a few miles, and when the helicopter got close enough, he turned the engines off again to play the same hide-and-seek game. Signorino's voice coming from the radiotelephone sounded worried, but loud and clear. "Mario, can you hear me?"

"I can hear you clearly, Vincenzo."

"What's going on? Are you alright?"

"I haven't got a clue, Vincenzo. The only thing certain is that we're in big trouble. The buggers have sent everyone but the submarines!"

"I know, Mario. I'm at Etna with friends, and we can see you through the binoculars."

"Are we visible from there?"

"The others because of their lights, but we can make you out from the trail when you're speeding. But why have you stopped?"

"That's the plan; I can't explain right now."

"How bad is it, Mario?"

"Awful."

"What are you going to do?"

That question had been plaguing Mario's mind as well, who frowned, not knowing what to answer. The helicopter flooding them with light all of a sudden simplified the situation.

"I'll tell you later, Vincenzo. I have to go. They've seen me!"

He pushed the levers and accelerated, zigzagging to get away from the blinding light, which was also guiding La Spina right at them again. He pretended he was making for the port and everyone fell for it, except La Spina's captain, who, like he'd read Mario's mind, turned right and cut off his route to the open sea. Swearing, Mario motioned the men to hold on, and just before he was trapped, veered sharply, risking capsizing, and zoomed past the patrol boat's bow, on his way to the open sea, while he counted three bullets lodging into his boat.

He was doing fifty miles an hour, darting in random motions to avoid the helicopter, and increased his distance from the patrol boat, got to the open sea, and hit the swell. The speedboat was gliding spectacularly from wave to wave, but its speed was reduced from the swell and La Spina was within shooting range again.

Swearing, Mario tried a channel blindly and managed to maintain his headway. But he lost any hope of getting away in the open sea, and turned back again to re-enter the bay as soon as possible. The horrible engine roaring was driving him mad, messing with his thoughts, and his excessive speed in pitch dark blinded him from anything in his path.

Guided only by his instinct, Mario raced like hell, with his heart in his mouth, trying to increase his distance from the patrol boat, and hoped for a miracle to save him. Amidst the pandemonium, it was difficult to hear Signorino. Mario beckoned a lad to hold up the microphone for him and shouted, "Go ahead, Vincenzo."

"We can see you again, Mario. Why have you come back? Over."

"It's going from bad to worse. I'm losing speed out at sea. I was forced to come back in."

"The helicopter is leaving you. It's going!"

Mario could also see the helicopter moving away, along with the other patrol boats, which gave up the pursuit and proceeded to limit his space, positioning themselves accordingly. They were certain that he would fall into La Spina's clutches, which was after him with all its might, so close that it would be impossible to lose him. The possibility of escaping the enclosure they'd trapped him in was just a dream now, and Mario howled, grinding his teeth furiously. "I've been cornered for good, Vincenzo."

"What are you going to do, Mario?"

It was the second time he'd asked him, and the answer was becoming ever more difficult.

"I don't know. But I'm not going to sit around waiting to get caught. I'll fight to the end."

"Good, Mario. I'm counting on you; that's why I've placed a bet."

"I didn't quite get that, Vincenzo. Repeat. What did you say you've bet on?"

"On your not getting caught."

"Are you serious? I'm drowning here, and you're gambling me away?"

"Make sure you get away without handing them the boat, and, trust me, Mario. The wager is going to be worth your while!"

He saw through the patrol boat's fake zigzagging in good time, but pretended he'd taken the bait. He turned suddenly in the opposite direction, escaping the trap and gaining a few more meters, just until the next trick, which was won by La Spina, approaching him at around a hundred meters. The misleading twists and turns continued with shared success for a long time in the darkness of the bay. Mario was so overwhelmed that he kept cursing the patrol boat captain using every obscenity he'd ever heard, only to conceal his admiration for him.

The boat felt like it was flying, as it hardly touched the water, and Mario was trying to forget the maddening sound that dismantled his thoughts and prevented him from finding a way out, as the captain read his move again and narrowed his field even more. Fuming at the prospect of daylight finding him in prison, Mario pushed the levers with all his weight and was terrified by his quick glances at the temperature in the engine caps, which were filled with smoke. He was able to increase his distance from the patrol boat for a few more minutes, prolonging the time he had to decide how to escape.

His frightened Sicilian passengers cowered to take cover, holding on to whatever they could. Mario's nod to get closer to him revived their hope, and they jumped up. Screaming to be heard, Mario showed them the temperature and fuel needles on the dashboard. "The engines will not last for much longer, and we're running out of petrol. I'll try to get us out, but I can't see anything. Do any of you know the area we're in?"

Peeking at the patrol boat approaching again, the short bloke took a step forward and clasped the seat. "I know, Mario. It's near my village."

"Look to your left. Is what we've just passed a beach?"

"I don't understand."

Mario pointed at the spot in the gloomy land silhouette. "Is that a beach over there? Do people swim there in the summer?"

The confused Sicilian nodded. "Si, Mario."

"Is it rocky?"

The lad seemed at a loss. "I don't remember…"

Mario prepared to ask again, but the patrol boat that had almost reached them, forcing him to cut the conversation short. "Never mind. Just hold on tight!"

The patrol boat was less than fifty meters away when Mario feinted for the last time. La Spina thrust its bow forward; he swerved, zooming past it, and headed straight for the beach in full speed. The patrol boat recovered its course quickly, but had fallen behind by a few meters and was running out of time.

With one hand on the wheel, Mario jumped off the seat to get ready, adjusted his body, and stretched out his other hand to slow the boat down, but didn't make it. They rapidly crashed on land with a horrible judder, which propelled him sideways onto the cabin. The boat continued to waggle on its way through the sand, until it suddenly stopped, while the sharp sound coming from the engines sucking up sand in full revs signalled the alarm for Mario, who was struggling to get on his feet.

"Jump! It's going to explode!"

La Spina had stopped a hundred meters away. The beam from La Spina's headlight,, pointed at Mario, helped him find his way as he jumped onto the sand. He saw the track in the sand the boat etched for more than thirty meters, all the way to the bushes, where it got stuck.

Thanking his lucky stars, he started following the Sicilians, who'd already been running through the bushes, when he realized something was wrong. Only after running for twenty minutes, though, did he notice that his left shoulder, which was moving uncontrollably, had been dislocated.

He found it odd that he couldn't feel any pain and kept running, stooping in the dark, struggling to get away from the danger zone. He followed the Sicilians' clatter of feet while the branches were whipping him, and his left arm was rotating.

His local assistant's voice ahead warned him to be careful; Mario looked up, but his chest got caught on the barbed wire. He pulled back, groaning, and as he was feeling his body, he heard a sound from his elbow. He turned to see what'd happened when he heard the second sound of his shoulder slipping back in, and that's when the throbbing pain started.

They made it a good way through the vegetation when a thunderous bang brought them to a halt. Looking behind, they saw the blaze that illuminated the entire area, passing the Mario Lafitte into history.

Giovanni in the old fiat located them easily in the wild and dodged the roadblocks while driving without lights through the dirt roads and fields. They arrived in Catania at daybreak.

...

In the photograph on the front page of the local newspaper, which Signorino handed him with a grin on his face, it was clear that all that was left of the speed-boat was a smudge on the sand. The caption mused over what the mysterious speedboat had been transport-ing, whether it was guns, drugs, wanted fascists, or just cigarettes.

The answer came in the next page by the pompous cap-tain of La Spina, who was smiling in a small photograph, expressing his disappointment that for no one had been arrested. He was certain that this had been an important illegal activity that had been intercepted thanks to his well-trained crew and the coordinated actions of all the forces, which had liaised impeccably.

The bombshell that made Signorino laugh came at the end of the statement, where the captain praised the pur-sued coxswain's abilities, expressing the desire to meet him in person. There was a more detailed report on the inside spread, plus two photographs of Mario Lafitte at sea in daylight, taken from the air. In one of them you could read the boat's name, while in the other you could clearly see Mario's assistant gesticulating indecently at the air-plane taking their pictures.

"This is great. The bugger was so impressed, he wants to meet you. You're famous!"

Mario stopped reading the newspaper and looked at him, dumbfounded. "I can't understand why you're so pleased. Have you forgotten we've lost the boat?"

"Mario Lafitte may have perished gloriously, but we haven't lost it. Maybe you've forgotten the wager..." and winked at him, chuckling.

The bet more than compensated Signorino for the dam-age, but the commotion in the area would take ages to die down. They wouldn't be able to work in their position for months, and the new boat he'd ordered wouldn't be delivered before summer.

The prospects for the following months looked grim, but they didn't seem to worry Signorino, who was calmly driving the Porsche, singing along Bruni's latest hit.

"It's March, Vincenzo. If we miss two months, it's the end of our season."

"We're not going to miss anything, Mario. We'll work with another squadra, away from here, and we'll be back when we're ready."

"And why would the others want us meddling in their business?"

Putting on his happy face, Signorino took a cigar out of his pocket and offered it to him. "Because we're the best, my man. Everybody wants to work with us. Until then, though, come with me to Como while you're waiting for your arm to heal.'"

With an extremely stern look, the old doctor informed him that his arm wasn't badly damaged. However, until the swelling had subsided, he was to rest completely, so Signorino invited him to Como.

CHAPTER 13

With the Alps in the background, near Lake Como and just outside the beautiful city, Signorino's double life was blossoming in the elegant two-story villa, with a rose garden on the outside and fair Sonia with their five-year-old son on the inside.

Mario spent a week resting in the mountain air and his arm was mended. Signorino, for his part, enjoyed playing with little Bruno and his stunning mother, made a few phone calls, promised them he would be back in ten days, and went back to his official family, to organize the business.

Having been used to living with her husband for short periods of time and spending most of her time alone with her son, the lovely Sonia was very pleased that Mario would stay behind so she would have company. They quickly became friends, enjoying long walks and endless talks.

Sonia would listen very keenly to Mario's entertaining stories about Greece, laughing her heart out with the

Greeks' obsession with smashing plates. But when the conversation touched on marriage issues, her mood would change; her eyes became melancholic, and she stared at her wedding ring pensively. Mario wondered if Sonia knew the truth about the other wife, but he never asked her.

It had been twenty days and Mario was starting to get bored, when Signorino returned to Como in high spirits, full of affection for Sonia, gifts for young Bruno, and new business plans.

"We're going to work high, Mario. La Spezia, Carrara, Genoa, wherever's more convenient, but around there."

"That's very far from our waters, Vincenzo. I've never been there. I don't know anything about the area."

"You'll have a month to familiarize yourself. Is that enough time?"

"But it will be summer in a month's time."

"So much the better, because you'll pass for a tourist this time."

"How? Backpacking and hitchhiking?"

Signorino took a sip of wine to control his laughter and got serious. "This is a special occasion, Mario. You'll be in charge of a yacht."

"Are you serious? Contraband in a yacht! Sweet! Go on..."

"Nothing major happened. I was looking for people to work with somewhere, but the vessel coming into my possession has freed us from..."

"How did you come upon it?"

"That's not important. What matters is that we legally own it, and we can work alone again, like we're used to. There are some problems, though."

"What sort of problems?"

"The boat is wooden, fifteen meters long, with a top speed of thirty miles."

"With thirty miles, Vincenzo! It's like we're inviting them to catch us. I'll get picked up on the first trip!"

"Not if you're a tourist. A luxurious yacht is not suspicious, especially in those parts."

"Even if they're naïve in those parts, a Greek bloke in an Italian boat is bound to raise suspicions."

"Impossible, because it's going to have a Panama flag, and you'll be the owner. Do you like the setup?"

"I can't say it doesn't sound appealing. But, Vincenzo, it would be difficult for a delicate, wooden boat to withstand the contraband demands. It's going to get damaged quickly. Have you thought about that?"

"You're right, and it's going to be a shame, because it's so quaint. But the only thing I care about is to finish with the cargo. Let's hope the boat can be saved as well. Agreed?"

"You said I've got a month, but you haven't mentioned where I'll be staying."

"At the moment, the boat is in the marina in Carrara, but perhaps you shouldn't stay there; we don't want to attract attention. Pick another place, as long as you stay in the area."

"Like where?"

"Genoa, San Remo, Monte Carlo—anywhere you want."

"Did you say Monte Carlo? Can I stay there?"

"Of course, Mario! You're a tourist, owner of a yacht. You can moor wherever you fancy!"

The radio presenter announced it was midnight, gave a short news bulletin in French, then Italian, and then continued the program with songs as the approaching city's reflection intensified. Mario counted the lead lights,

consulted the map in front of him, and smiling content-
edly with his impeccably chosen route, slowed down and
turned the volume up to enjoy the music.

Being used to travelling the way he had, the five hours
it took him to arrive seemed long, but went by pleasantly
and effortlessly, without jolts and noise. A smooth-sailing
craft, the Perla, with diesel engines that didn't yield high
speed, yet worked like well-tuned clocks, was much better
than what Signorino had described in Como.

He was stunned when he'd first seen it, white and gorgeous, and when he got on board to check out the interior,
his heart sank. "It's a doll, Vincenzo! Don't you feel sorry
for it?"

"I've told you Mario. I don't care about the boat. I care
about the cargo."

Mario grimaced and pointed at the luxurious lounge.
"After a couple of loadings, all this is going to be ruined."

Signorino turned to get off the boat, laughing. "Until
that happens, make sure you make the best of it."

The Monte Carlo radio station presenter declared that
the time was one in the morning as he was slowly entered
the brightly lit port with the numerous, glitzy cruise ships.
He started looking for available space to moor, and he
soon discovered a suitable spot. He couldn't fit, however,
so he set out searching again. He circled around to no avail
and stopped, troubled, in the middle of the port. The current was dragging him to the left, on the edge of the jetty,
toward a huge cruise ship. He threw his cigarette in the
sea and started the engines to continue searching, when
he finally saw in the shadow of the big ship the elusive gap
that he could dock in.

Thanking his luck, he moved quickly and reached the buoy. There was no one at the pier that late to help him, and for half an hour he was moving back and forth, trying to tie up, paying the price for his refusal to take with him the assistants Signorino had offered.

By the time he'd finished, he was panting like a dog. It was almost two in the morning. He was so tired he couldn't see straight, and he slept like a log.

"Monsieur, Monsieur, si'l vous plait."

The gold-coated clock in the cabin opposite his was showing it was past ten when Mario opened his eyes, and, before he quite knew where he was, the voice in his dream was heard again.

"Monsieur..."

Smiling awkwardly, two lads clad in freshly pressed uniforms were trying to detect any sign of life through the smoky grey portholes and didn't notice the half-opened cabin door next to them.

Revealing only his head, as he was in the buff, Mario addressed them in English. "I'm here."

The lads were startled, but didn't get annoyed; on the contrary, when they looked at him, their smiles widened.

"Bonjour, messier."

Mario returned the smiles; he protruded his naked arm through the half-open door, shook their hands and pulled it back.

"Parlez-vous français?"

Mario made a disappointed face and retorted, "Speak English?"

It was the Monegasques' turn to get frustrated, and Mario felt for them.

"Parla Italiano?"

The lads sighed in relief. "Si, si, certo!"

The naked arm came out again, extending an envelope, and the port officials looked at each other puzzled.

"What's this?"

"My papers; isn't that what you're after?"

"Mais, non, monsieur, no papers."

"What, then?"

The man who offered to explain lowered his eyes and took on a morbid look, like a funeral director. "Monsieur, you have to leave."

"Leave? Go where?"

Without lifting his eyes, the lad pointed at the marinas with the endless lines of yachts.

"Over there. You're not allowed to stay here."

Mario opened his mouth to start complaining but immediately thought better of it, as his eyes met for the first time the substantial red letters on the jetty that covered more than thirty meters and informed all those with sight that the space was reserved exclusively for the Hydrographic Office of Monaco. The second look revealed that the same was written on the buoy he'd tied up at night, as well as on the red vessel moored to his right. In need of time to improvise, he asked them to wait for a couple of minutes until he got dressed. He closed the door, put his clothes on quickly and took the binoculars to examine the port in daylight. A minute later, he was certain there wasn't enough room even for a dinghy and he recognized the imposing, lonely yacht that had caught his eye the previous night, about fifty meters away from him, with the name Christina emblazoned on its bow. Pretending he was still buttoning up, he walked out of the cabin, smiling and suave, and patted them on the back in a friendly manner. "I'm really sorry, mates, honestly; but I can't move."

"But here, Monsieur, is Hydrographic Office property."

Mario looked around him, laughing.

"Don't you think I know that?"

"Then why are you here?"

"I didn't want to put the other boats at risk. There's a fault with the rudder."

"Oh, I'm so sorry, Monsieur. We can get an engineer to repair it, but we'll have to tow you in another position."

Mario pushed the fridge door shut with his back, handed out beers and shook his head forlornly. "I'm afraid, mates, that you're going to have to bear with me for a day or two until the insurance company assessor gets here. If the boat is repositioned now, it might get more damaged and I won't be compensated. As for engineers, if I need any, I'll be assisted by the Christina."

Being unversed in Greek-style teasing, their eyes popped out.

"Do you mean by monsieur Onassis?"

Mario shrugged. "Of course. We're very well acquainted."

Brimming with servility, the lads in the crisp uniforms spent half an hour with him, had another beer, asked Mario to promise that he wouldn't delay more than two days, gave him their card in case he needed something, and left smiling and contented, while Mario praised his ingenuity, and stayed put for three months.

Always low profile, Jimmy, Onassis's bartender, discreetly tapped on the door when he saw through the window that Mario and Cindy were in the lounge. He waited for Mario to wave him in. Like every time he saw her,

Jimmy silently declared his admiration for the English girl via hand kissing, picked up the Corriere della Sera from the coffee table, and went to sit out of the way, on the bow sofa, with a long face.

Short, middle aged, with sparse hair and an amiable countenance, Jimmy, originally from the Ionian Islands and with more than twenty years of working for the mega-ship owner, had travelled the globe on board the Christina. He knew the favorites of all the magnates he'd served and had been present in discussions that had influenced the lives of thousands of people. But he would never open his mouth unless he was addressed, and when he went out to the port to unwind, he was alone, closed to himself, surreptitious and mistrustful of everyone.

From the first days of his arrival in Monte Carlo, Mario had noticed the solitary, elderly bloke, who was peeking as he was passing by the boat, and a week later, when he found out who he was, invited him on board to have a drink and a chat. Forced to walk past him every day when leaving or returning to the Christina, the surreptitious bloke got used to the presence of the Perla, pepped up a bit, overcame his apprehension slightly, and went on board. Trying not to scare him off, Mario let him believe that he was from a well-off family, told him as many of Moustachy's jokes as he could remember to cheer him up, and in a couple of days managed to relax him.

Jimmy started spending all his free evenings with him and Mario discovered, among other things, that the old bartender lusted after young ladies, loved gambling, and adored tequila. That was when young Cindy entered their lives and messed him up even more.

That afternoon the heat was scorching, so even the tourists who usually killed time by staring at the luxurious yachts were few and far between. Mario had been routinely sunbathing on Perla's flying bridge with the sprayer on to keep cool, when he got up to re-fill his glass with ice cubes and heard the girls giggling.

He'd heard the same voices earlier and had absent-mindedly watched the shapely young ladies in the hats following the same route, like other yacht-gaping tourists had. Then they walked past him laughing and continued on until the beginning of the red strip leading to the Christina. They briefly admired the Greek tycoon's ship, turned around to head back, and Mario forgot about them until he heard the laughter again. The young girls were having fun striking silly poses in the Perla's back windows, thinking they were alone, and were startled when Mario appeared suddenly in front of them, applauding.

There was an awkward moment, but then they burst out laughing, and when Mario tinkled the glass with the ice cubes, the English girls looked at each other for a minute and got on board, running with excitement. The attraction between Mario and the green-eyed Cindy was instant. A few hours later and a little straight-talking, things were settled, and the girls came to an arrangement and kissed each other goodbye. Emotional but happy, one went off to continue her travels, and the other, the green-eyed girl, stayed on at the Perla. A pretty and cheerful girl, young Cindy happily obliged when it came to Mario's sexual yearnings, cleaned up his bachelor mess, and breathed new life into his plan to draw Jimmy out and set his scam in motion.

A fluent English speaker, the old bartender wiped his drool, licked the salt, and downed the tequilas, delighted to have found a young bird to brag about his glorious past as a servant to the well-heeled. The young girl in the imperceptible bikini opposite him was crossing and uncrossing her legs gracefully, raising his blood pressure, without giving a damn about his stories. She was smart enough, though, to show admiration, exclaiming every now and then, turning old Jimmy red-hot.

With eyes gleaming from lust and drunkenness, the bartender kept recounting every night the comings and goings of all the powerful people that had been aboard the Christina. He talked to them about the charming but stand-offish Jackie and her caprices, about the humane yet tough side of Onassis that everybody dreaded, about leaders with kinks to make your flesh creep. The interminable, spinster-like gossip was gnawing away at the hours, and Jimmy was downing the tequilas with the lemons that bloated his belly.

Cindy's ability to show interest was admirable, but Mario, who'd been hearing most of the stories for the second time, started getting bored and wondering if it was worth putting up with him. Then Jimmy mentioned the night swimming in the Christina's pool and burst out laughing.

"What's so funny, Jimmy?"

Jimmy was holding his belly from laughing so hard, but he wouldn't take his eyes off Cindy's thighs.

"They swim in the buff. Do you know how funny they are?"

"And how do you know, Jimmy? Do they skinny dip in front of you?"

Jimmy gestured at Mario to give him a minute to catch his breath, coughed five or six times, and, struggling to control his drunken laughter, explained to them that it was done through the engine room by few initiated members of the crew, who had found a way to entertain themselves by peeping at the butt-naked leaders of the world. While they were enjoying their carefree night swimming, splashing like toddlers in the warm water of the lit-up pool, they were being watched above their heads. Mario welcomed the shiver going through his body and pulled his chair closer.

"Are you serious, Jimmy? And they are clearly visible?"

"Crystal clear, mate..."

"Have you taken any photos of them?"

Jimmy looked at him, astonished, like he'd been shot, swallowed his laughter, forgot his drunkenness, and turned into the surreptitious confirmed bachelor again. "Photographs?"

"Just for the fun of it. Hasn't it crossed your minds?"

"Joking with photographs when you're working for Onassis is not an option. Heads will roll!"

It was obvious that the old bartender got scared, and, facing the risk of wasting the effort of so many days, Mario decided not to push him further at that point. He asked the English girl to join them and quickly changed the conversation topic to the cocktails the tycoons used to ask him to mix, since that was Jimmy's strongest point and he was deservedly proud, as most of them were his own concoctions.

Keen to sample a new VIP flavour every night, the crafty Cindy turned on the charm with giggles and poses that made the bartender squint and in a matter of days, managed to squeeze out of him closely guarded secrets about most of the celebrities' favorite drinks while Mario was writing the recipes down religiously in a notebook, convinced that it was a future investment.

The famous couple's skinny-dipping in the yacht pool under Monaco's starry sky revived the elusive dream and reminded Mario of the paparazzi in Lefkas and their struggle to secure the speedboat that would transport them to Scorpios to try their luck.

In the exchange market, photographs of naked Kennedys amounted to security for life, like winning the lottery. But he was just as likely to score as the numerous paparazzi in Lefkas' port who were armed with huge telephotographic lenses. They had been pleading, promising money, or threatening Mario, who remained indifferent until Pierre the Frenchman came along with the best offer.

Pierre had offered commission if they succeeded and as an advance payment, the eccentric, fallen Austrian princess who was a famous porn star in Europe and was dying for adventures in her spare time. They had been going around Scorpio in the Clara for four days looking for the big break, and Mario, when there were no guards to ward them off with a shotgun, approached the island as much as he possibly could to help Pierre. The porn star princess was getting excited, but to no avail, and the Christina sailed off. The porn start departed for Athens for the premier of her new film, and Pierre embraced him sadly to say goodbye, told him C'est la vie, and gave him his card.

"What should I do with your card, Pierre?"

"Take it, Mario, you never know."

Mario put the card away with his other papers and forgot about it until that evening, when the tequila worked its miracle and loosened Jimmy's tongue. Mario had spent five whole days out of his life, a case of tequilas, along with hours of talking and patience, until on the fifth night, with Cindy's valuable assistance, the asphyxiating siege yielded results.

From early on, the bartender seemed to be at odds with himself. He drank an ocean of shots with them on the Perla before accompanying them in the car to the casino. Totally wasted, at the last corner before they had arrived, he decided to confide in Mario. "Well, it's OK; I've arranged it for you."

Mario was thrilled. "What have you arranged, Jimmy?"

"I've made plans with Manolis, the third engineer. You remember him."

He'd met them on the first few days, when he'd joined them on their drinking binge a few times.

Mario's impatience was choking him now. "Well?"

"At the end of the week, we're expecting the boss to get back from America. By Monday, he says, he'll set it up for you because he likes you."

Trying not to jump for joy, Mario straightened the car that had crossed into the opposite lane and patted Jimmy on the back. "You're the man, Jimmy!"

"That's fine, thanks. Just remember to tip the lad for his services, and, God forbid, make sure no photographs end up in the hands of those greedy paparazzi, because we'll get it in the neck."

"That kind of thing doesn't really happen, Jimmy. Don't worry."

"Of course it does. Do you know how much money the paparazzi make with such photos?"

"Really, Jimmy? That's so wrong. The world is full of bastards."

"Exactly—that's why I'm telling you. Be careful!"

Mario looked at him slightly offended yet dignified. "We don't care about money, Jimmy. We only care about friends."

That night, Mario got hammered early in the casino and observed the tradition of losing all his money. When he embraced Cindy and Jimmy while heading home, however, he was humming happily, while the familiar punters at the back of the casino were making the V sign, certain that he'd finally won. The unscheduled meeting with Signorino the following night, though, ignited the fuse that would blast the plan that Mario had been working on for so long, wasting his money, his patience, and his tequilas.

Mario was so enthralled by the photographic treasure hunt that he completely forgot about the contraband and the squadra and put off contacting Signorino until the next day. He set off early with Cindy and Jimmy for a ride around the picturesque Monte Carlo. They dined in a posh restaurant and around midnight headed for the casino again to end their evening.

Mario threw the keys to the hired Renault at the parking attendant, who rushed to remove it. Mario took Cindy by the hand and they climbed the steps to the imposing entrance, glancing enviously at a Maserati, next to a black Porsche, which reminded him of Signorino. Confident that he would own a similar car in a matter of days, he entered the hall smiling. Suddenly, a familiar voice coming from his right nailed him to the floor, flabbergasted. "Eh, Mario, finalmente!"

Polished and primped like the cover model of a magazine, Signorino embraced the dumbfounded Mario tightly, while next to him in a bow tie and unshaven as always,

Giovanni was smiling, showing his yellow teeth. Jimmy and Cindy further back were watching, ill at ease.

"You disappeared, Mario, and we were worried. You haven't rung for an entire week."

Mario rushed through the introductions, mentioning only names, excused himself for a minute to Jimmy, took Signorino by the arm, and led him further down, to the small lounge that was empty. Signorino sat down, sighing, examined his well-groomed fingers for any wear under the lamp light and started complaining about the unbearable heat that had scorched them as they looked for the Perla all morning. When they'd finally found it, there was no one there, so they decided to wait for him at the casino, certain that he would drop in at some point. And they hadn't been mistaken.

Mario let him whine for a while about the money he'd lost at the roulette and then cut him off to explain the situation. A descendant of generations of swindlers, Signorino listened carefully, and it took him less than a minute to get the picture.

"I see, Mario. You're right; it is serious indeed."

"Isn't it worth fighting for?"

"When's Onassis coming?"

"In five days."

Truly disappointed, Signorino shook his head.

"I'm afraid you don't have enough time. That's when we're starting."

"What are you saying? We can't even extend it for two or three days?"

"No, unfortunately not, Mario. The dates are fixed. Monday to Friday, you have to clear as much cargo as possible. Not even a day, Mario. I'm sorry."

"Maybe I can still make it, though."

"I hope so. In any case, tomorrow I'll send your two assistants to show you the post, to start getting ready."

Their chat didn't last longer than ten minutes. Signorino gave Mario whatever chips he had left and kissed him good-bye. The Italians got in the Porsche to leave, and Mario rushed to get a place at the roulette table and to avoid Jimmy's interrogation, who was looking at him suspiciously again, until he'd come up with a credible excuse. Betting without concentration, he lost his chips quickly, but put on his indifferent smile, like he did every night. "Can we go, now? I feel a bit tired today and I've got some things to sort out in the morning."

Jimmy kept looking at him funny, but did not say anything until they got on the car. "Look, Mario, you don't have to answer, but I'm curious. Who were these people?"

Mario turned around, joining his eyebrows innocently. "Are you talking about Mr. Vincenzo? Haven't I mentioned him before? You're right, I forgot to. He works with my father."

"Your father? What does your father do, by the way?"

"He has a desk full of telephones and closes deals. You know the type!"

Steward on the ferries his entire life, Jimmy managed in his own way with his incredible cocktails to become a top bartender, but he'd never heard of working with telephones. Neither could he have met Mario's father, Mr. Michalis, the fisherman, so he just nodded, but it was evident he hadn't relaxed.

"Who was that brute with him?"

Mario looked at him reproachfully.

"You should be embarrassed, Jimmy! Calling him a brute. He's the president of the workers' union. You know, the ones we employ."

"President, eh? A strange bloke, anyway. While you were talking to the gentleman, he was looking around him like a crow, without uttering a word. He looked like a gangster to me."

Mario stretched out worriedly, but started laughing with the joke, told Jimmy to stop watching American films before he'd completely lost it, and was still laughing when he stopped before the red carpet to drop the bartender off.

"Well, my friend, Jimmy, au revoir until tomorrow, and don't forget: stay away from gangster movies!"

The old bartender, laughing, climbed on the Christina to go to bed, and Mario, who thought he was out of the woods, rubbed his hands excitedly and hugged the green-eyed girl. "If this falls into place, my little one, we'll continue your holidays in Mykonos!"

The English girl's emerald eyes echoed their joy in a gaze that Mario would never see again.

CHAPTER 14

Mario filled the glasses and looked anxiously at the shiny bald patch behind the Corriere della Sera. The silence and the bartender's long face—until he'd had some shots—were normal, but the unusual hide-and-seek behind the newspaper seemed odd. When he noticed that Jimmy was completely indifferent to Cindy opposite him, then his stomach churned, and he became really worried.

From her lounger, the young girl shrugged, puzzled, in response to his inquiring look. Mario sighed, moved closer and tried to look nonchalant as he dangled the shot in front of Jimmy's nose. "Come on, Jimmy. Drink your tequila. At the end of the day, if a boat has gone down, it's Onassis's, not yours!"

Jimmy put the paper aside, swallowed the shot in one go, like pill, and, without saying a word, his face dropped again. Mario swallowed the urge to slap the sweaty, inviting bald patch, grimaced, and tried again.

"If someone has died, let us know so we can mourn him together, Jimmy. That's what friends are for."

With his head bowed, the bartender waited for Cindy to re-fill his glass. He looked at it for a while like he was weighing it, then in a single move poured the content down his throat, gurgled, and plucked up the courage to look Mario in the eyes. "Mario, stop lying. There's no need. I know what's going on."

Although he had prepared himself for such a development, the blow was really strong for Mario.

"What have you learned, then?"

Jimmy pointed at the lounge clock with his head.

"They'll be here any minute; I told them they would definitely find you here at this time."

"Who, Jimmy?"

Jimmy smiled sadly, downed the third shot, and leaned back.

"Your assistants, the Italians."

Mario opened his mouth, but he regretted it, and Jimmy went on.

"They came over to the Christina to ask us if we knew where you were, and he had a little chat."

"And where was I?"

"You should know. Didn't you go out for lunch?"

Mario was already cursing himself mercilessly for his stupidity at forgetting about the assistants Signorino was going to send and looked at young Cindy furiously, for she had insisted they had lunch again at the remote seafood tavern she loved so much. Proving Onassis's unerring judgement, who had kept him as his personal bartender for decades, Jimmy handled the situation like a genuine nobleman, without aggravation or spite. So, after his sixth tequila shot, he loosened up, as always, and his countenance softened. Demonstrating his superiority to the dazed Mario, he acknowledged every poor man's right to keep trying for the big money, comforted him, wished him the best of luck in his next endeavour, downed his tenth shot, and when Mario's assistants arrived, he got up to leave, reeling.

At the door, he shook Mario's hand and hugged him, moved. "I must admit that during the past three weeks I had a lovely time with the two of you, but I guess you realize that I can't visit again."

"I understand, Jimmy. That's alright. Now that the whole thing has gone sour, we can't be seen together. But why not work together on the scam? It's a lot of money, Jimmy. Aren't you tired of being a servant?"

The bartender extended his arms, laughing. "Look at me, Mario! What should I do with all the money now? It's only going to get me into trouble."

He left for the Christina, staggering, and Mario brimmed his glass with whiskey, watching him fade away down the quay, along with his dream.

...

Shrieking, Cindy rushed to catch her hat before it ended up in the water, while the Italians were showing their fists threateningly as the red helicopter flew noisily above their heads and landed gently on the Cristina's heliport. Mario looked on sadly at the famous couple hastily greeting the servants, who'd been waiting under the sun, and then disappeared in the coolness of the luxurious interior. The helicopter switched its motor off, restoring peace in the area, and relieved Mario's tense nerves. He groaned and halfheartedly pressed the buttons to start his engines.

He headed slowly for the open sea and spent six hours making sure that the position his assistants had shown him was suitable. He recorded the marks he needed, and when he returned late in the afternoon, he noticed that Onassis's helicopter was missing. So is Onassis, Mario thought. Jimmy, though, did not show up at all for the rest of the evening, dashing Mario's last hopes to get the con going.

Around noon the following day, the helicopter split their eardrums again. It unloaded its precious cargo and stayed put until dusk, when Mario sailed off again to check his post at night. He got back to the port past midnight and the helicopter was still there. The yacht seemed dim, but the music and laughter reached his ears clearly, along with the glint of the illuminated pool, which attested to the magnates' high spirits. Missing his big chance stung even more now that it was paraded in front of him.

The two double whiskeys didn't help much, and when he finally drifted off, it was almost dawn. The helicopter took off unusually early, and he woke up swearing. Before he even had a taste of his coffee, the helicopter returned, dropped three people off, and left right away, only to land again a few kilometers further down, on the roof of an imposing building, which also belonged to Onassis.

Mario sent one of the Italians to let Signorino know that they were ready to work at night and hugged young Cindy, who was smiling though her sparkling, green eyes were filled with tears. He held her briefly in his arms, whispering in her ear tender words he didn't mean, promised to write to her, kissed her as convincingly as he could, and handed her over to the other Italian to accompany her to the station.

During the course of the day, the bustle intensified at the Christina as the trucks with the supplies were arriving one after the other. The helicopter completed the same flight many times, transporting various people, and the preparations continued with the same fervor until late in the evening, when the floating mansion was illuminated, justifying its reputation. The supply trucks were replaced by dark limousines and expensive sports cars, which took over the quay space.

Mario poured himself a drink for good luck and flicked through the notebook with Jimmy's cocktail recipes. Fancying that it might worth a lot of money if it ended up in the right hands, he put it back in the drawer, grinning, and started the engines to leave. As if having planned a send-off for him, the Christina's band picked that exact moment to start its set with his favourite tune.

The celebrity party in the floodlit Christina was in full swing as Mario steered slowly toward the exit. He half-circled to avoid the lights and slipped into the dark open sea for the Perla's baptism of fire in the contraband, while the laughter coming from Onassis's many high-profile guests, which could be heard from afar, seemed to be mocking him.

He didn't have any trouble finding the ship at night. The difficulties began when he tried to approach it and realized that the Perla, compared to the special boats he'd been working with until then, was uncomfortable and inappropriate for the swift moves their work demanded, as it was hard to steer. Having had enough experience to anticipate the problems he would soon encounter, he asked the crew to hang more fenders. However, although it wasn't windy and the sea was almost waveless, every time it touched the hull, the wooden yacht creaked loudly, forewarning disasters.

Mario kept it as steady as he could and signalled reluctantly with the flashlight to start loading. Perla was a delicate boat, designed for cruises and romance. It couldn't possibly withstand the contraband's roughness. The flying boxes of cigarettes that pounded its deck with the force of gunshots destroyed whatever stood in their way. In a matter of few minutes, the beautiful yacht had been transformed into a bombarded barge.

Mario's heart ached for the former beauty who was being trashed, but he nodded when asked for permission from his assistants to complete the destruction needed to accommodate the extra cargo. A little later, the luxurious lounge and the bedroom were floating away in the Mediterranean.

The Perla set off for the shore at twenty miles per hour, which made it an easy target for any patrol boat that might have located it. Externally, though, it was still the elegant, white yacht with the foreign flag, among so many others plying the resorts of the area and did not raise suspicion. He got to the unloading post without any incidents, and Signorino, who had been waiting for him, didn't seem particularly bothered about the boat's sorry state. He reminded him again that he only cared about the cargo, but agreed that it would be best to avoid the ports in such a mess.

He was halfway through his second voyage to the ship when the automatic pump's red light came on suddenly on the dashboard. He jumped up, interrupting his thoughts. An inspection with the flashlight confirmed that the creaks were not empty threats. The Perla was letting in water that the pump was handling at the moment, but he knew that things would get worse.

His first logical thought to return and have it repaired was instantly rejected as impossible, due to time restraints. The calm sea was under no obligation to wait, and Signorino's words, who didn't care at all about the boat, were still ringing loudly in his ears.

He put the spare pump on standby, designated shifts for the Italians to watch the water level, and continued his course in the dark, with a sense of being on a fool's errand. The three hours he'd slept on the ship weren't enough, and in the morning light Perla's condition looked a lot worse. The cracks were more than he'd originally thought, and water was coming in from all sides, but still at a pace the pump could deal with. At sunset, the southwesterly winds picked up, making things worse.

Mario edged the ship with extreme caution and started loading. It was impossible to avoid the two knocks on the bow and the same number of hair-raising squeaks that widened the existing cracks even more created some new ones and forced him to start the auxiliary pump.

When he set sail for the shore, the Perla was listing like a tanker and was hard to steer, while its maximum speed dropped to twelve miles, increasing Mario's insecurity. The Perla finally made it to its destination, shattered, with pumps screeching. Mario was ready to walk away. It was one of the few times that Signorino seemed upset about something, but it didn't last long. Signorino made arrangements with one of his men to go with Mario and hide the boat a few miles away and said he would be waiting for them there. He was getting into the car when one of the pumps stopped and made him return, bucked up.

Mario knew straight away that the pumps had reduced the water level because the boat was rid of the cargo weight and was lifted, resulting in less water getting in. He also knew that this was temporary, and explained that to Signorino, who chose to disregard it.

Having tight deadlines and pressing obligations, the Italian pleaded with Mario to have another go—even with half the cargo. Mario didn't have the patience for all that begging and finally relented and agreed, although his whole being was warning him against it.

The southwester was not very strong, and the waves it generated would have been a joke for any other boat. For the half-wrecked Perla, though, it was like climbing the Calvary; one third of the way in, the squeaking resumed, and the auxiliary pump started again. Seriously worried, Mario reduced the revs, and he hadn't even covered a mile when the creaks became lengthier and louder, while the main pump, after having coughed twice, fell silent forever.

Two times more water was busting in uncontrollably, and the auxiliary pump, still holding out, was fighting for its honor. Mario motioned reassuringly at his assistants, who didn't believe him, and turned his bow with difficulty to return to the Carrara port.

He thought he had time to get there, but as he was getting closer, gradually losing speed, the left engine stopped together with the pump. In the following hour, which seemed like a century to Mario, the crippled Perla, filled with water, managed to reach the first boats in the port, as the last working engine died as well. They rushed to jump on the first fishing boat to escape the current, leaving behind them the sinking Perla. They were pulling ropes and leaping from one boat to the next, until, soaked and exhausted, they got to the pier at the first ray of light.

They scurried to jump quickly over the fence before the guards realized they were there. Then Mario halted suddenly, determined to turn back, when he caught a glimpse of the half-sunk boat in the distance. Changing his mind, he climbed over the fence again and got to the street, cursing himself as usual.

The squadra lads waiting for him in the car covered him to protect him from the cold and found his swearing quite normal. Mario didn't explain to them that he had been swearing neither for the boat he'd lost nor for his expensive clothes, but for Jimmy's cocktail recipes he'd forgotten in the drawer.

With bitterness as his permanent companion after the Perla fiasco, Mario's holiday in the northern Aegean was a complete letdown, not at all resembling what he'd been dreaming about. As the days went by, the sense that he was wasting his time for no reason was becoming increasingly stronger, tainting his last reserves of good will. When Signorino rang for the third time, he asked Mario to be patient.

The summer had ended ingloriously, the same as the money from his last trip. He began distancing himself from the business and making plans for the future that didn't involve the contraband. The period when he'd been crawling around Piraeus begging for any position in a potato freighter now seemed remote and meaningless, while the constant extravagant partying, the designer clothes, and the high life in exclusive locations had lost their luster and became a chore.

During the three and a half years that young Mario had been quenching his thirst for adventure and experiencing unprecedented thrills, living every day like it was his last, he had spent bucketloads of money. His conviction that he wouldn't live long enough to enjoy it mobilized his friends and family to try and help him. Using various excuses, every time they saw him, they wrung money from him to set aside. As a result, two years later, Mario, without even knowing, had saved enough to start a new business on land, without anyone to boss him around. He began dreaming again.

On the first day of September, Signorino rang again to find out how he was getting on and to ask him again to be patient, but Mario's unusually apathetic tone troubled him, and he changed approach. A highly instinctive man, he sensed the danger of losing his coxswain and did not give Mario much room for arguments. He used all his powers of persuasion, speaking quickly and curtly, ruling out any objections, stressed that Mario was expected in Catania by the end of the week, hung up the phone, and left Mario staring at the receiver in confusion.

Things in Sicily were still unclear, and Signorino was striving to get organized, but it was obvious it was going to take time. It had not been necessary for La Spina to return to the area, as for quite some time the contraband had been slow, almost nonexistent. New, ambitious people had sprung up in the trade and others had retired, while the officials on the take had been transferred to continue fiddling elsewhere. There was a rush of organizational activity that would give work to hundreds of people, but there was a characteristic delay; it was the same story for the new boat, which wouldn't be delivered until October.

Signorino's offer to lend him to some friends in another squadra and maximize his time came at the right moment, just as he was getting frustrated. Without thinking about it much, he let Signorino arrange the details and left for Messina. The post was quite convenient, and the summery calm seas were still holding out. Mario assisted in a few trips and the cargo was completed, unlike Signorino's preparations. In an effort to gain more time, after putting him up at his house for a few days, he loaned him again, this time to Trapani, on the other side of Sicily.

The gigantic inflatable boat they gave him for the job may have been ideal for other kinds of activities, but for the specific task of carrying cargo in open sea, it would have been completely unsuitable, that is, if the only patrol boat in the area hadn't received a hefty backhander to look elsewhere for a month.

For the two weeks he transported the cargo, the Finanza's patrol boat maintained its blindness religiously. Everything went well and the voyages on the inflatable boat resembled scouts' expeditions. Mario, too embarrassed to ask about his fee, left the matter to luck and returned to Catania, where an overjoyed Signorino finally informed him that they would start the following month.

"And the boat?"

"You'll collect it from Lefkas on time. Tonight I'll introduce you to the rest."

"What do you mean?"

Signorino popped the champagne open with an exclamation and poured it, laughing.

"More people are involved, Mario. The business has expanded."

"Go on, tell me."

"There's been a reshuffling on the street, and most people wanted to work with us. I've taken on some good ones."

The clinking of the crystal glasses was celebratory, and Mario felt bad because he couldn't share the enthusiasm. "It wasn't bad when we were working on our own, Vincenzo. Do you think that if we become a rabble, we'll be working better?"

"Nothing changes for us, Mario, except for the turnover, which is going to be bigger. The business has doubled, therefore so has the profit."

"Double business? How?"

"I've booked double the cargo."

"Really? How about boats?"

Signorino looked sadly at the ash from his cigar that had fallen on the floor.

"We're friends, Mario. That's why I wanted to talk to you. You'll be on your own in this cargo. Make sure you train someone, and when we're done with this job, we'll have a second boat. Do you see how much I need you now? You have to be rested. What do you say, will you make it?"

Hoping that the cheerful sound would clear his worries away, Mario chinked Signorino's glass. "I've done it before, haven't I?"

The ambitious launch of the new squadra with double the cargo and more people involved demanded an adjustment period that Signorino hadn't worked out properly. The job started badly, vindicating Mario for his dislike of mobs. Meetings on top of meetings and endless private discussions to assign tasks and responsibilities finally came to fruition. The new team was well organized, with development prospects, but they took forever, and by the time Mario sailed off in the new boat from Lefkas to meet the Salonica in the open sea, November was about to wave goodbye, and the weather was beginning to show its teeth.

"Hello, Mario, I've heard a lot about you. I was told that you used to work with Charis. He must have spoken to you about me. I'm Lefteris!"

Mario could not remember anyone by that name, but smiled anyway, and shook his hand. Ever since Moustachy had called him the month before to let him know that he'd quit the Salonica—because he'd got tired of waiting and left for Spain—Mario hadn't been very keen on the prospect of working with a captain he hadn't met before. He'd even thought of quitting himself momentarily. But then the deep gratitude he felt for Signorino prevailed; he vowed to give it all up for good as soon as he'd completed this cargo, thinking (mostly to put himself at ease) that it was likely the new captain was as good as Moustachy, and probably not as bonkers.

Tall, handsome, athletic, and poised like an admiral, it would be hard to live up to Moustachy's panache.

Bafo's replacement did not impress Mario.

"This is Simos."

The lad who averted his worried gaze from the waves and shook Mario's hand had a forced smile on his face, sweaty palms, hadn't shaved for a week, and had it not been for his foul stench that made you nauseous, you would have never remembered him.

"Nice to meet you, Mario. What do you think of the weather?"

The "admiral" looked at him in disdain and winked at Mario.

"He's worried about the weather, but he'll get used to it. In a few months, I will have turned him into the best captain in the Mediterranean. Isn't that so, Simos?"

The reassuring pat on the back was not enough to boost the morale of the trainee captain, who started staring at the horizon again. Mario, in turn, introduced them to Nicholas, his new assistant whom he was training for the new boat. He then left him on the bridge to get better acquainted with them and went down to the bow to inspect the cable before it got dark.

The boat was following smoothly and comfortably on the waves, but to be on the safe side, Mario loosened the cable ten more meters and went to help the Corfiot who was struggling to move the barrels.

"And Burglas, the cook, what has become of him, Spyros?"

The Corfiot tightened the ropes, groaning, looked at Mario, and laughed.

"Can you imagine? All of a sudden, he told us that he'd put enough aside to open a tavern in Port Said, and the following day, he got on a plane and left."

"I haven't seen Phaedo, though, either..."

Spyros made a sad face and turned his attention to the next barrel. "Poor Phaedo had a hard time. He took off as well, and the jokes stopped for all of us."

"Why, what happened?"

"His aunt died, and his little sister was free to roam the hotel beds again. As you can probably understand, he rushed off to try and sort her out.'

"And who replaced them here?"

"There's a young lad in the engine with Makis. But he's too young for this kind of trouble, and he'll probably quit soon. You've seen the other one on the bridge."

"Who, the filthy bloke?"

"That's him!"

"What's up with him, Spyros? Does he like being a cesspit? Why doesn't the wanker take a shower?"

The Corfiot abandoned the ropes for a minute to laugh his heart out.

"He's too scared!"

"He's scared of washing? Are you kidding me?"

"He's afraid of getting into the shower in case the ship capsizes and he's trapped inside. Ever since we set off, he hasn't slept in his cabin once. He spends all his time on the bridge."

"And they're trying out this chicken-shit for a captain?"

"We're out of trump cards, Mario. Had I known this would happen, I would have left, too. The new guy, your trainee, what's he like?"

Mario looked at the sea and smiled half-heartedly. "He can swim..." He fell silent for a moment and then went on, as if talking to himself. "It's alright, he's a fast learner. We'll see..."

"Oh, well, it's not a big deal. Besides, Captain Lefteris isn't much better."

Mario sprung up in shock. "Are you serious? But he was..."

"I'm telling you, he's a knobhead. Didn't you see his flipping maneuvers while he was trying to tow you?"

Mario had seen them and wasn't much impressed, but had thought it too soon to jump to conclusions. "That means we're in trouble, Spyros."

"You don't say…"

In Valetta they were joined by the squadra member who was to attend the cargo, and a young Maltese lad who would complete the crew. Simos, the first mate, rushed to get rid of his stench in the comfort of the hotel, and when he was shaved, the well-bred mamma's boy that emerged was still frightened, but at least not so smelly. Neither did he ask to leave for Greece, as Mario had hoped; instead he shut himself in his room and didn't leave the hotel until they sailed off again.

On the contrary, Captain Lefteris—being as proud as a peacock—hooked up with the young Maltese as his guide, and for the three days he disappeared, he tried his best to make himself known throughout Malta. Then he returned to the hotel broke. He stayed for a few hours, long enough to convince Makis, the engineer, to lend him some money and disappeared again to continue his parade, until he'd blown that money, too. On their seventh night there, he entered Mario's room in a rush, dampening his spirits, and headed straight for the bottle of whiskey. "I reckon we should leave tomorrow."

Mario attempted to hide his displeasure and gave him a dark look.

"That's what you think. Poseidon, though, has different plans."

The captain made a gesture reminiscent of an admiral again. "There's nothing wrong with the weather, Mario. It's fine."

"What are you talking about, Lefteris? If fresh gale is fine for you, for me it's hell. What do you think you're piloting, Lefteris? The Queen Mary? You're piloting a small motor ship. And how about the speedboat? Do you think I can travel in such weather?"

"By the time we get to the port, it will have settled, Mario. Let's not waste another day. The weather is calming down, I'm telling you."

"The barometer has hit bottom and is still going down; the weather forecasts are expecting gales, and you're telling me it's going to calm down? Why do you want to go so badly, Lefteris? Because you're skint? Leave on your own. I'm not moving if the weather doesn't improve."

Captain Lefteris let Mario push him out without protest, but lingered in the hallway. "Anyway, we have to go. They'll be waiting for us."

"Chill. No one is waiting for us."

"You don't understand. They're expecting us tomorrow. I've rang them."

"Are you serious? You've mobilized the squadra without asking me?"

The captain turned around hurriedly to depart, and Mario kicked the door shut to resist the temptation of smashing his head in with the bottle.

CHAPTER 15

The only thing differentiating that December day from the previous was that they were at sea.

The wind was blowing as strongly, bashing the small islands, the clouds continued their crazy races in the sky, and in moderate visibility the roaring, frothy waves constituted a warning against those who were about to defy them.

"Where are we going, Mario? That jerk is going to drown us!"

Mario steadied the cable in the distance he wanted the boat to be towed at, looked around him, grimaced, and didn't answer. He'd known since even before they left Valetta what a reckless voyage they had embarked on, but when he realized that the weather hadn't improved at all, the alarm bells in his mind started signalling retreat.

The expression on their contraband colleagues' faces who'd been watching their departure almost made him quit. But being held responsible for the unnecessary squadra mobilization and putting Signorino in a difficult position with his new partners were two things he really didn't want to happen.

Staring in his eyes, the Corfiot was pushing for an answer to appease his worries. Mario, however, didn't have an answer.

"Look, Spyros, whatever we say will be nonsense. Now we're here, we have to play; there's no other way. Only take care of the boat. Don't lose sight of it. If anything goes wrong, we'll need it."

He left the Corfiot looking at the boat pensively and went upstairs to the bridge. Without even a smidgen of his conceited smile, Captain Lefteris glanced at him fleetingly and turned his attention to the bow. Makis the engineer gave him a friendly nod, and Simos the first mate, sitting opposite with his head lowered, didn't even know Makis was there.

"What's going on, Simos? Is there something wrong with you?"

Simos's eyes betrayed his anxiety, and when he spoke, his voice coloured it even more. "What do you think of the weather?"

"The same as you do: it's shit; but what's the matter with you?"

Simos bent down again mumbling something about his stomach and remained curled up. Mario went downstairs to take a hot shower and counted three pens' worth of sheep until he got some much needed sleep. When he returned to the bridge a few hours later, the setting was the same, except for Makis, who was sitting with an open book in front of him but wasn't reading.

"Well, Mr. Commander, what's going to happen now?"

Captain Lefteris pretended not to have sensed the ironic tone. "What do you mean?"

"I'm trying to say that not only has the weather not settled, but you also have a sick man on board. We'll just about make it to the position shortly, but it'll be useless. Can you tell me what you're planning on doing, or haven't you got a clue?"

"What should I do? Turn back?"

"Don't we have to run for port? Can we do that in Italy with the cargo holds full of smuggled cigarettes? We can only go to Valetta."

"I'm not going back to Valetta. We left only a few hours ago. We'll make a fool of ourselves."

"Not we. You'll make a fool of yourself, but do you have any other choice?"

"Of course I do. We'll wait a couple of days, and if it doesn't calm down, then we'll go back."

"Do you mean to say that we'll be smashed around like octopuses for forty-eight hours to save your pride? Have you thought of Simos?"

"There's nothing wrong with Simos. He'll be as fit as a fiddle tomorrow."

The crouched first mate groaned desperately, but the conceited captain went on, ignoring him.

"We'll keep north-westerly, which is convenient for the weather, and we'll turn back in the morning. Don't tell me you're afraid of a little fresh gale, too?"

Mario barely controlled his burning desire to snap the captain's neck.

"I'm worried about the boat, Lefteris. If the waves get any higher, it's going to be in danger, and we might lose it for no reason. Do you get me?"

Captain Lefteris sipped his coffee and turned his gaze to the ceiling. "I remember in Japan, when I was second mate in a tanker and we were caught in a cyclone..."

"Go to hell!"

Mario banged the door behind him, preferring to jump overboard than listen to the conceited captain's stupid story, while Makis had the same reaction a few seconds later, albeit displaying a lewder linguistic repertoire.

The special forecast broadcasted by the Valetta radio station announced an expected deterioration of the weather conditions in the next twelve hours, instructed the sailors to be vigilant, advertised the Maltese traditional hospitality, and send an infuriated Mario back to the bridge.

"Have you heard the weather forecast?"

"I have—so what?"

"Turn back now, while there's still time. Stop messing around because if the forecast is confirmed, it will be impossible to get back without losing the boat."

"You're taking them at face value, aren't you, Mario? Don't have such great confidence in them. We'll turn back in the morning, like we've said. We'll head straight for the position to work, and you'll be left with the whining in the end."

Trying in vain to appease his terrible anxiety, Mario spent the rest of the day in his cabin browsing Italian magazines; every once in a while he went to the bow to check his boat, which, although was quite loosened to move freely, seemed to be having a terrible time during the sharp bumps that tightened the cable, whereas the splashing waves landing on it left their foam behind, making it even heavier.

The gloomy dawn found them twenty-five miles north-west of Pantelleria, in the worst conditions, which vindicated the Maltese meteorologists and threw the conceited captain into confusion, while the panic-stricken first mate was writhing in pain. With the weather in broad reach, the pitching, old Salonica continued on its agonizing, futile course in the wild Mediterranean, dragging behind it with great difficulty the poor speedboat, which disappeared in the waves and re-emerged heavier than before, constricting the cable dangerously and distressing Mario, who was desperately looking for a way to protect it.

The only hope of saving the boat faded away, as time was passing by, and the wind and bad weather wouldn't let up, contrary to Captain Lefteris's obstinate expectations, who was totally at sea, just like his ship, unable to find a solution to the problem he alone had created. He systematically avoided meeting the engineer's eyes to avoid an outburst, and only said what was necessary.

It was almost dusk when Mario, with his assistant and the Corfiot, soaked from the sea water and shaking from the cold, looked on, choked with terror, as the speedboat was hit by a huge wave on its side. It sank and before re-emerging was hit by the next forceful wave trying to finish it off. The boat's stern dipped, causing the bow to stick out sky-high, like it was asking for help. Then, within seconds, it went under completely and disappeared, as if it had never been, making Mario's blood run cold and paralyzing him just for a second, until he pulled his knife and rushed to the cable.

On its free fall into the abyss, the submerged boat was dragging the Salonica's bow with it. The taut cable had been reduced to half its original length, so when Mario touched it with the knife, he didn't have to try hard. It was immediately severed and followed the virgin boat to the bottom of the Mediterranean, a sacrifice at the altar of a selfish idiot. The Corfiot and his assistant approached Mario to comfort him, but he wouldn't let them. He asked them to leave and stayed there alone for a long time, staring at the spot where his boat used to float just minutes earlier and forcing himself to accept the loss and regain the necessary composure before he saw Lefteris again.

It was well into the night and he was trembling when he dragged his feet to the superstructure, holding on to whatever he could so he wouldn't be thrown overboard by the heavy knocks. After so many years at sea, it wasn't until that night that he felt nauseous.

Freed at last from the weight of the trailer, the relieved Salonica was braving the storm better, and despite the propeller's frequent emergence from the water, the engine kept revving up again quickly. The ship looked like it could handle the strong gale, but the voyage was pointless now, since they were crippled by the loss of the speedboat and had to go back, thwarting the plans of hundreds of people who had been waiting for the cargo in order to make a living. His anger turned into exhaustion, and when he went up to the bridge later, he didn't even feel like swearing at Lefteris to let some steam off. It was a good thing, too, given Lefteris's weak condition. In the dim light his mug was as white as a sheet, and he was crouched; during the jerks, he was losing his balance, stumbling, and as if he was being been woken up abruptly, he was getting alarmed and grabbed the parapet again. They were all there, clinging on to whatever they could, nestled away from the cold, and no one was speaking.

The engine's roaring mixed with the howls of the wind was making the men's silence even more unbearable, and Mario regretted joining him. He pulled a bottle out of the box behind the wheel, looked at the captain disgustedly, and turned to leave for his cabin. Makis took a step forward and stopped him at the door. "Where are you going? Are you leaving?"

"What does it look like?"

"Don't go. Please stay. We have to discuss this."

"There's nothing to say, Makis. That's it; it's done. We have to start over."

"I'm talking about now, Mario. What do we do now?"

"I'm just the coxswain, and I don't even have a boat anymore. Are you asking me?"

"And whom should I ask? Captain Wanker over there?" Makis shouted this on purpose, but the captain didn't seem to have heard, and Mario looked at him funny.

"Hey, you, Lefteris?"

Lefteris didn't react at first, but then turned slowly and cast his eyes somewhere on his chest.

"Will you finally tell us what you're planning to do, Lefteris, or you going to surprise us again? And, just to be clear, do you know what you're doing?"

The captain's voice was hoarse and faint, forcing them to strain their ears to hear him. "Now the damage has been done....We'll go back in the morning..."

"Why not now?"

"As soon as there's light. I don't want to risk the ship as well."

"I'm asking you again, Lefteris. Are you sure about what you're doing?"

"At daybreak...so we can see."

Lefteris resumed his pathetic expression, turned to his front again, and stopped talking. Mario shrugged at troubled Makis, stuck the bottle in his jacket, and left the bridge in a hurry to avoid putting his already tense nerves to the test. Bumping from bulwark to bulwark, he returned to his cabin, picked up some objects that had been spinning noisily around the floor, drank some whiskey to get warm, and then lied down, wedging his feet in the parapets to resist the roll, with his mind wandering back to Catania.

It was easy for him to imagine the confusion in the squadra and Signorino's apprehension, who would be moving heaven and earth to retrieve his cargo, until captain Lefteris got the guts to request a phone call from Malta Radio and report his damage. An old hand in this business by now, he could guess the additional problems and new delay the lack of speedboat would cause, but this time he had no intention of waiting.

Certain about Signorino's reaction, who would try to appeal to his better nature as usual, he decided to fly from Valetta in secret and ring him from Greece later to explain. This thought calmed him.

He didn't think he could sleep, but the idea of going home sweetened his soul, calmed his nerves, and his eyelids got heavy. The final glance at his watch informed him that it was almost two o'clock in the morning and reminded him of the tenth of December, which was about to dawn. Mario smiled tiredly, wished himself happy birthday, and fell asleep.

'Wake up, Mario!'

The loud voice and the sharp knock on his side felt like he'd been electrocuted.

"What is it, Nicolas? What's wrong?"

His assistant's tense face and his whistling breath did not allow any room for positive thoughts. "They need you upstairs, Mario! Quick!"

He barely managed to balance himself in the strong roll, got ready in seconds, and rushed to the deck door, meaning to climb from the outside and save time.

"Don't! Not the door!"

Nicolas's shout behind him was heard together with the screeching of the half-open iron door. Mario was about to ask why when he saw the huge wave above his head. He froze for a moment, but then shut the door again instinctively before the gigantic wave shook the boat and threw him to the floor. "What was that, Nicolas?"

"We've fallen into a cyclone, Mario!"

On the bridge, even Simos was on his feet and the prevailing confusion was bordering on panic as the men kept moving around to balance themselves, while they were all shouting simultaneously at Lefteris, who had crouched even lower not to see anything, as if losing his view would ease the burden of his responsibility. Mario pressed on, stumbling from one to the other and screamed in Lefteris's ear. "Don't be such an idiot, Lefteris. It's going to hit us on the side! Are you blind? Why are you not turning back?"

In utter confusion, Lefteris answered to himself. "A hurricane...twelve Beaufort...Not even in the Pacific..."

"Never mind all that, Lefteris. You have to head back, don't you see? What the hell have you been taught? Can this old, rotten, wreck take the weather on the bow sides? Are you such a fool? If it doesn't fall into pieces, it's going to capsize, and we'll meet the boat at the bottom of the sea. Wake up!"

"Shall we not wait until the morning? It's dangerous..."

"The first light is an hour away. I think we should vote on this."

With few words and even fewer objections, his proposal was voted unanimously. Mario replaced the young Maltese on the wheel and made quick arrangements with Makis, who left for the engine room. They stopped talking, and everyone's attention turned to the raging sea, desperate to locate the low wave that would allow them to turn. The wind roared, and their bow disappeared in the watery hills, which gave them the creeps. The minutes had been going by in nerve-wracking tension until the experienced Corfiot, who spotted the first suitable wave, started yelling. "There it is, Mario, it is coming!"

Mario signalled the mechanic to rev up and kicked the helm windward. The Salonica quivered dangerously as it hit the next wave with higher speed, but managed to lift its bow to the surface again and started turning. The low wave that crashed forcefully on their side shook the ship like an earthquake, filled the superstructure with water, and halted their turning, knocking their breath out of them.

The men could see the looming, high waves approaching, and it looked dead certain that they would cap them, yet the old craft made it again, and the heavy waves hit them on a broad reach, accelerating the rotation they were after.

The risky turn was successful, and the crew started cheering excitedly. Mario smiled in relief and released the helm so it could unroll. The wheel spun quickly and kept rotating. Then the clunking sound of a chain breaking erased Mario's smile.

He shook his head to send the nightmare away and grabbed the wheel and stopped its spiralling, but it didn't take him long to realize that it was no use, and numbness spread over his body.

The desperate groan from deep inside his soul sounded dissonant amidst all the enthusiasm, and the men looked at him, confused. Mario got off the stool and furiously kicked the wheel.

Reacting to a bleak reality, the men kept watching in disbelief the uncontrollable wheel spinning. Then the Corfiot tried it, and Mario broke the news to the rest. "Unfortunately, lads, we're adrift."

In the ensuing mayhem, Makis was breathing deeply to remain calm while most of them were running in various directions, screaming. Simos, the first mate, groaned loudly and curled up again in his corner, whereas Mario poured a bottle of whiskey down his throat to control his heartbeat. Only captain Lefteris, clasping the handles, did not react at all. Encouraged by the captain's composure, Mario called Makis so they could go over and talk to him. When they got next to him, though, and Lefteris turned the other way, they instantly knew the reason of his seeming coolness. Captain Lefteris had shut himself off, jacking his responsibilities in, refused to converse with them and kept answering in monosyllables, without even facing them.

They were being pressed for an immediate solution, so they couldn't afford to waste any more time with him. Makis's suggestion to slap him was dismissed, and when they walked off in disgust, Lefteris sighed and turned in on himself again.

"Leave him, Makis, there's nothing we can do. What do you think?"

"If we don't do something soon, we'll capsize."

"What can we do? Think of something. Can we fix it?"

"Now? In this state? I don't know. We have to break the bulwarks to see where the chain is, but we don't know for sure what's happened, and it would take hours."

"Is there anything else?"

"There are some tackles in the warehouse. If we hook them up on the bow and all of us hoist it, maybe we can steady it...I can't think of anything else right now..."

"Hurry, then. Get the tackles."

The risk of being swept over was immense, but Makis and the young Maltese managed to hook the tackles up quickly. They were immediately divided into two parties and, pulling at the ropes like crazy, they balanced the ship. However, this undertaking under such circumstances was extremely straining, and as if that wasn't enough, it also started raining.

Mutated into millions of needles, the rain was hurting the men, who had been working bent to protect themselves from it, while their teeth chattered from the cold. Their brains were numb, struggling to keep focus; the bow was plummeting into the abyss, churning their guts; and then rising up again, as if intending to fly away.

One of the teams misjudged the weather, almost costing them the dreaded capsizing, and they had to waste a lot of energy to restore the ship's balance. There was no more room for error, so the idea to send Mario on a lookout to give them directions was met with universal agreement.

Mario helped himself to a bottle of Johnnie Walker and climbed to the highest possible point where he could stand safely, above the water tank. With his feet tangled in the wire that held the tank in place and his palms meshing his eyes, Mario directed them confidently, knocking back whiskey regularly to keep warm. The taxing effort was halved, which allowed the freezing men to rest at the first glint of daybreak.

The first light of that miserable day exposed their hell. Their visibility had improved, though, which boosted their morale, and they repaired the damage on the right winch, which was about to break. The first mate dumped the rope on the others, pulled himself back, twisted his body haphazardly on the iron ladder, and stayed there in the water, doubled up in pain. Just then, Captain Lefteris mumbled something no one understood and headed for the bridge. Underneath the tank, Makis cupped his hands and called out to Mario. "We have to get organized."

Mario nodded, and the engineer showed him the temporary fix with the winches they'd come up with for the helm. He mustered a smile.

"Isn't it nice? Now it's more workable..."

"Until when?"

Makis withdrew the smile and crashed back down to reality, dejected.

"I don't know...we'll freeze..."

Mario shouted at the men to hoist on the right and turned to Makis again. "What do you think? Shall we make a mayday call?"

"Definitely, Mario."

"How's the engine holding up?"

"It's OK for the moment, but it got too much water earlier, and still is. The cargo's also a mess. The boxes are floating."

"The first mate?"

Makis glanced at his side and sighed.

"The poor lad is coughing up blood."

"Go quickly, and tell Captain Wanker to make a may-day call, and make sure he doesn't give the wrong position. Then take a look at the wheel again, in case there's something we can do."

The movements of the men that had remained at the winches eased up a bit, after the rain had stopped and Mario could see better, but the storm persisted, unabatedly. The wind was whirling and disorientating, the waves resembled mountains, and their fatigue was evident; but they all continued hoisting without complaint, except for the Corfiot, who hadn't stopped cursing Lefteris even for a minute.

Time was painfully slow in the piercing cold, and Mario looked at the almost-empty bottle in his hands in astonishment.

"Keep going on your own; I'll only be a minute."

"What are you talking about, Mario? Have you lost your mind?"

"I have to wee, Spyros. I'm bursting."

"Why don't you pee over there?"

"Because it's going to land all over you, Spyros."

The Corfiot did not hesitate to decide. "It's no big deal. Get it over with."

Mario looked hesitantly around him. Then he turned to the side as much as possible, trying not to aim toward them. His good intentions did not help much, though, as the wind was ensured an equal quantity of urine sprayed on all of them, while the disgusted men were wiping their mugs with the back of their hands. But no one uttered even a word of protest, and the distressed Mario turned his head the other way to avoid seeing them until he'd finished peeing.

Makis came back a lot later, exhausted, with a torn sleeve and the morale of a man on death row. "Things are not looking good, Mario. The holds are filled with water, the dunnage is not visible in the engine room, the doors are smashed...and we're letting water in nonstop."

"Is it really so bad, Makis?"

"We're sinking, Mario. At this rate, we'll last a few hours, but we're going down for sure."

"How about the chain or the wheel?"

"Forget about it. Nothing can be done."

"Has Lefteris asked for help?"

"He already had before I got upstairs, but the wanker made a mistake, like you thought he would. He says it's moving too much, and he can't read the instruments well. He's still trying."

A drone from above interrupted their discussion, and their hearts beat faster with anticipation. The small airplane circled around and returned flying lower. The crew started yelling and gesticulating, but the airplane flew higher and stayed there, watching them.

"At least now the idiot won't have to find the position. They will give it."

"Where are we roughly, Makis? Have you seen the radar?"

"We must be around forty-five miles southeast of Sardinia. Only seagoing tugboats can travel this distance in such weather. Even so, it would take them a few hours to get here."

"Will we be afloat by then?"

Makis heaved a sigh again and looked at the airplane circling high in the sky.

"I hope so, Mario. I have two young children, dammit!"

"They'll send helicopters, Makis. They'll be here in an hour at the most."

"Let's see."

They were looking at the sky when the pilot of the observation aircraft decided that his mission had been accomplished and vanished into the clouds toward Cagliari. Makis got upset. "Hey man, he's gone!"

"It's for the best, Makis."

"For the best? The bastard abandoned us. We had some hope…"

"What's the point of having him circling above your head if he can't help you, Makis? If I'm meant to get drowned, I don't want to be a spectacle for anybody."

"We have to hang on at all costs, Mario. We have families…"

"You're right, call that skiver Lefteris to get down and help; besides he's useless up there now."

Lefteris had to be pushed by Makis to go down, and when he got to the bow, he looked entranced again. Even though he was forced, however, he did help the freezing lads take a breather. With a wet blanket under his arm and a full bottle in his pocket, Nicolas, his assistant, skidded twice but managed to climb to the tank. He squeezed up next to Mario and unfolded the blanket to cover their shoulders. The blanket suddenly swelled like a jib, slipped from his hands, and got stuck high on the funnel. Mario took a sip of whiskey and gave him a hug. "I'm really sorry, mate."

"What for? It was just an old blanket."

"I'm not talking about the blanket. I'm talking about the hassle."

There had been many suitors when he was looking for an assistant with potential to make a mint, some of whom very experienced sailors, but Mario had decided to take the inexperienced Nicholas with him, shaken by his run of bad luck. The previous year his father had passed away unexpectedly; within months his mother, who hadn't come to terms with the loss, followed, while his younger brother's condition drastically deteriorated. The three months he had to spend on a public psychiatric hospital damaged him even more, and the private clinics' fees were a burden his older brother, Nicholas, could not lift, given the pittance he was paid.

"It's not your fault, Mario."

"I dragged you into this mess."

"You did it to help me, Mario. I'm the jinx. What's happening? Have we got any hope?"

Mario took another sip before he answered. "I'm not going to lie to you, Nicholas. We're friends. If the helicopters manage to fly in this wind, we'll be saved. Otherwise, it's going to be difficult."

"You know, Mario, I don't give a toss about myself. Maybe it'll even be for the best, but I'm thinking of the kid, and I'm going mad...He'll be left all alone...Who's going to look after him now?"

Mario coughed and pretended he was clearing the salt out his eyes to hide his tears. "You'll take care of him again, Nicholas. Are you crazy? We're not dead yet, we'll fight, my friend."

Flashing with anger, he asked Makis to take his place and rushed to the bridge. The images he collected on his way up left little doubt as to the Salonica's imminent demise, as it was being knocked about, crippled, prey to the storm, its holds steadily filling with sea water. Its bow, which was almost permanently submerged, made him visualize the way it was going to go down, and he shuddered.

The bridge doors had smashed the hooks that had been holding them in place, and they were opening and closing raucously, while the scattered maps and instruments everywhere heightened the feeling of desertion. Mario leaned to his side to dodge a stool that was coming straight at him and grabbed the microphone.

"From the Salonica, mayday. Can anybody hear me? Over."

Holding his breath, he released the switch and the ravaged bridge filled with strange noises and interference. Then, all of a sudden, a voice was heard from a distance, yet crystal clear.

"I can hear you, Salonica, I'm from the Attica. From the Attica. I don't know if you've heard me. Over."

"Hello Attica. I can hear you clearly, thank God. Can you tell me if you know what's happening? We're a mess here. Over."

"Hang in there, Salonica. They're on their way. Over."

"Who's coming? Over."

"There's a Russian freighter near you, and it's coming. Over."

"When will it get here, Attica? Over."

"It won't be long; it's close to you, close to you…"

"Have they got the position? Over."

"It's OK. They got it from Cagliari, from Cagliari. Helicopters have taken off from there, too. Over."

"Did you say they've sent helicopters? When? Over."

"They're on their way, on their way. I have contacted the ministry in Greece; they're making arrangements as well. They're making arrangements, too. I don't know if you understood me. Over."

Mario looked at the microphone, so moved he almost kissed it.

"I read you, Attica, I read you. Many thanks from all of us here. If it's OK with you, we'll talk again in half an hour, if we need to, in half an hour. I have to go and help now, tell me if you read me. Over."

"OK, Salonica. It's alright, in half an hour, in half an hour."

He found it odd that the men didn't get as excited as he had hoped. Their movements livened up, though, as well as their eyes, which turned to the sky to look for their savior amidst the clouds. But the thirty minutes passed by without spotting anything, and Mario headed swiftly for the bridge again before the Corfiot started whining.

Trying to be as reassuring as he could, the Attica's captain informed him about the Russian freighter and the approaching helicopters, asked him to hang in there for a little longer, since their rescue was a matter of minutes, and they renewed their appointment for the next half hour in case it was needed.

"This half hour has gone as well, Mario. Why aren't they coming? We're sinking, for fuck's sake, and the bastards don't give a toss. We'll drown like assholes..."

"Cut it out, Spyros, and try to keep it together now. We can't panic. Keep an eye; I'm going upstairs again."

"Shut up, you bastards. Shut up...our brothers are getting lost. Shut up, all of you—I'm trying to talk to them. I can hear you now, Salonica. Over."

Coloured by an overly dramatic tone, the Attica captain's screaming had an immediate effect, and the frequency cleared up on the spot. It also froze Mario's back, though, who got teary and disheartened, his voice sounding very tired. "Unfortunately we haven't seen anyone yet, Attica. We're still trying here, but we're running out of time. Over."

"Don't give up; keep fighting; now they're really on their way. They're flying now, they're flying now. Over."

"OK, Attica, alright, a wholehearted thank you from all of us anyway."

"I've confirmed it, Salonica, they're definitely coming now. Our people have come to an agreement with the Italians, and they've sent them. I repeat, hang in there. They're coming. Over."

"And the Russian, the tugboats?"

"The Russian is having trouble; it is difficult, and he's got the weather on the bow sides. The tugboats set off with the helicopters. Hold on for a little longer. Over."

"Barely, my friend, barely. Thank you."

Completely out of ideas, he stood staring at the radio in despair. Then he shuddered, nestled in the corner, and lit up a cigarette. He tried to concentrate on coming up with something to boost the men, but to no avail. He got up with difficulty and went outside to the stairs.

The final glimpse of the half-sunken deck caused his knees to give way. He slipped, but managed to regain control and got down to the bow like he was hypnotized. Fearing the worst, the men refrained from asking any questions.

They just looked at him and fell back into their despair, working mechanically like robots, having stopped scanning the sky for the savior ages ago. They relieved Mario of the duty of telling them things he didn't believe, however the first mate's stillness alarmed him and Mario leaned over him. "Hey, Simos, how are you, mate?"

Physically drained and indifferent to the water submerging him, the first mate raised his head slowly and let his eyes do the talking. Shocked by the imploring look and the dried blood on his lips, Mario turned to the others for comfort, but what he saw there dismayed him even more. Constantly stumbling, captain Lefteris could not perform any more; the Italian had dumped the rope and was holding his head, grimacing with pain; whereas it was obvious that the rest, who had taken the burden on, would not last long.

Climbing to his position above the tank felt exhausting and, panting, he snuggled next to Makis, who was shaking in spastic bursts. "Go, Makis, I'm taking over. Get downstairs and move a little so your blood can circulate. Go on, hurry."

"Does it matter?"

Punching him on the back to warm him up, Mario looked around. "I don't know...They've said that this time they're on their way. Anyway, if we do get away, we'll owe it to the lad from the Attica, who galvanized all of the Mediterranean for our sakes."

Shaking, staring blankly at the spumy peaks, Makis did not make any comments. A little later, the Italian pulled out completely, holding his head. Captain Lefteris slipped and landed on his face in the water, groaned, dragged himself to the iron ladder and laid down next to his first mate who did not understand anything.

The freezing, famished, sleep-deprived men who had remained at the winches looked like they wouldn't last much longer and were about to give up the futile struggle when a noise was heard from above. They instantly straightened up with new energy. For a few moments, they were searching among the clouds; then they saw it approaching, and suddenly despair turned into a triumphant shout by the exhausted men, who found the strength to jump for joy.

The military helicopter performed a reconnaissance circle high in the sky, then descended gradually, and continuously zigzagged against the storm to keep steady above the bow. The first attempt failed. It tried again, did better, and started hauling down the winch.

Clearly overjoyed, Mario yelled at the men to remain at the ropes. He jumped down, waited for a convenient roll, and burst into the flooded superstructure to get the ship's log and their passports. The water in the lounge was about knee high, yet the roll made it feel like the open sea, and the broken glass, along with the chairs that had been floating around, crashing on the bulwarks, had turned it into a death trap. As the wave splashed noisily on the opposite bulwark, Mario rushed inside, grabbed the purse with the papers from the cupboard, and barely managed to hold onto the fixed table.

On its return, the chilly water covered him completely, obstructing his breathing, but the table, working like a shield, safeguarded him from any injuries. Mario just about recovered his breath, waited a few minutes for the boat to tilt to the other side, and dashed for the exit.

Numb from the cold, but victorious, he went outside to the bow again, showing triumphantly the purse with the documents, and it seemed to him unfair that no one was paying attention. He raised his head high and barely saw Captain Lefteris as he was being pulled inside by the soldier.

"Where is he going, Makis?"

"Can't you see the scum? He cleared off first. Now that's a proper captain..."

"Why did you let him?"

"I didn't, the bastard. I was preparing Simos..."

"So?"

The engineer was about to explode. "He pushed me, Mario, the dirty bugger. He pushed me, grabbed the strap, and took off."

"Just like that, without saying anything?"

"He yelled that he was going up to make arrangements, and he'd come back down. He's putting us on as well. I'll smash his head in when I get up."

"Let him go to hell. Come on, let's get Simos ready again."

They had to try many times and almost gave up, when the roll momentarily let up and they managed to hold the strap steadily. Then they tied the Italian's belt around him for extra safety and motioned the soldier to hoist him. The helicopter started pulling him, but the wind carried him away, changing his position. Simos brushed past the stern mast and, as if by miracle, dodged the rigging. Mario sighed. "We've finally finished with him. Makis, get ready. It's your turn now."

"My turn? Why?"

"Because you're the only one here who has children. That's why."

"It's impossible, Mario. I'll stay till the end. What if there's a blackout?"

"If there is a blackout at this point in time, is there anything you can do? Tell me."

"No, but—"

"Stop talking. It's coming down."

Makis tearily put on the strap and went up easily. The Italian, though, who was next in line, was not as lucky. Even in the prevailing mayhem, his groan was clearly heard as his leg crashed on the rigging, dangerously swaying his body. Being a tough lad, though, he fought to hang on and didn't follow the fate of his shoe, which had disappeared in the spume.

"Why shouldn't I go up now, Mario? Who am I? The only wanker in the village?"

"What's happened, Spyros, do we have to go through this again? Haven't we agreed that those with families should go first? Stop whining."

A true man, Nicholas jumped in.

"Let him go up, Mario. It's no big deal. I'll stay with you."

"We'll do what must be done, Nicholas. Now help me catch the strap."

The half-sunk ship was not rolling like before, but the wind wouldn't let up, and the helicopter was taking a huge risk by remaining steady in its desired spot, as the swinging wire could get caught anywhere and throw them in the water.

After two failed attempts, Nicholas managed to catch it. He put it on skilfully and when he got a few meters high, he pushed comfortably up the mast, distanced himself from the wires, and reached the helicopter safely.

"I hope you don't expect me to wait for the Maltese as well."

"You'll wait, Spyros, like I'm waiting."

"You might get a kick out of torment, but what am I being punished for: Mario? And don't tell me that the youngster has a family and shit like that."

"Precisely because he is a young lad, Spyros. Have you no shame? Do you really have it in you to leave him here alone? What does it matter if you go up five minutes later?"

"Tell that to the captains that have abandoned us, not me. I'm just a sailor."

"So what? Just because you're a sailor, you have to be a wimp like Lefteris? I don't think you're like that, Spyros."

"Why have they only sent only one helicopter, can you tell me? If they'd sent two, we would all be gone by now."

"I don't know, Spyros. They probably thought one was enough. How should I know?"

"What do you mean you don't know. Haven't you been speaking to them?"

"Stop whining, mate, I can't take it any longer. I've told you what they said, and, besides, it doesn't matter now; we'll be leaving shortly as well."

The Corfiot mumbled something incomprehensible, but complied and stopped whining. He got up with difficulty, tried to steady himself, and took his place opposite Mario, covering more space so they could grab the strap, which was coming down like a celestial pendulum.

The young Maltese's eyes, which had a hot coal red tinge from exhaustion, gazed sadly at his wet coat, as Mario insisted he had to swap it for the life jacket. He didn't stop looking at it even after he'd been lifted off, but only until his arm hit the mast and transformed him into a spinning top for the rest of his ascent.

Mario watched him until he was pulled inside and then slumped down next to the Corfiot to take a breather.

"That's another one gone. You made such a big deal for nothing. We're next."

Breathing heavily, flat on his back and resting on his elbows, the Corfiot tried to say something, but was speechless. His groan resembled a death rattle and made Mario turn around, terrified. He too could not believe it—the helicopter gradually distanced itself by gaining altitude until it completely disappeared from view and headed for Cagliari.

"They're gone, Mario...They've abandoned us..."

On the last word, the Corfiot's voice faded. Mario shook his head, unable to fathom what had happened. He tried to get up, but his legs gave way and he collapsed in the pool of water. For a moment he stood still, then rose slowly to his knees and budged Spyros. "Come on, let's move further up. There's too much water here."

He stood, bewildered, staring at the spot where the helicopter had disappeared from view. The Corfiot did not hear a thing, and Mario shook him harder. "Come on, pull yourself together, we have to move higher, or we'll be swept away by the water here."

He pulled him with all the strength he had left and forced him to climb the five steps. He dragged him as far as the air duct and, without any strength left, lay on his back next to him.

"That was a shabby trick, Mario. They shouldn't have left. It's insane to dump people who you know are going to drown for sure....Am I right?"

Prematurely overwhelmed by guilt, Mario grabbed his arm. "Hold on, Spyros. I'm sure they'll come back."

"Do you think so? But when are they coming back? They don't have enough time; it'll be dark in two hours."

"They'll make it."

"Are you sure?"

Mario was not at all certain they would return or that they would still be afloat by then, but he didn't dare say it, to avoid hearing it himself. "Hang in there, Spyros..."

A little later, the Salonica's engine roar stopped being audible, accentuating the terrifying thuds and creaks, while the wind's lamenting howl among the masts became stronger. The Corfiot tilted his head toward Mario and twisted his lips in a grimace that barely resembled a smile. "But we've fooled the fucking weather, haven't we?"

Mario stopped rubbing his chest and looked at him. "If you say so..."

"I'm not kidding. The engine may have broken down as well, but the fucking weather has been fooled. I'm telling you, it can't capsize us."

"Is that so?"

"Yes, Mario, because now that we're adrift, it's not rolling as much. Do you know why?"

Mario knew where he was going with this, but played along.

"Go on, Spyros, tell me."

"Because we're already under water. It can't capsize us. It's impossible. Isn't it screwed?"

Their frozen bodies were shaken by laughter that was followed by weeping and coughing. Then they stopped, out of breath, and went silent. Mario let his hazy eyes wander in the grey sky, took out his cigarettes and was shocked when the wind blew the packet away, as his fingers had stopped working. Stiffened in half-closed fists, they refused to obey him, which he found odd. Then he thought it unfair and got angry, but his attempts to make them work again drained him and were to no avail.

He started feeling dizzy, and as the numbness spread throughout his body he no longer felt cold or afraid. His soul was gradually quieted, and just before losing sense of time, he remembered again that it was the day of his twenty-fourth birthday. He smiled. Then he was gone.

The young boy playing hide-and-seek with his brothers amongst the tall onion plants in the garden was laughing happily, while the young parents watching their children from the front door were beaming with pride. Then the young boy saw in terror that the rock he'd leaned on to climb had shattered and plunged him into the abyss along with it. The little brunette neighbour girl said yes, blushed, and smiled at him, the brand new bicycle was gleaming under the sun in the back yard, his mother covered him tenderly, crossed his chest, and kissed him on the forehead.

Mario knew he was dying but didn't want to open his eyes and fight for his life because the sweet serenity comforted him. So he didn't see the helicopter coming back. The pilot had to lower the aircraft significantly to make them out, and the visions were filled with noise. Mario fluttered his eyelids, annoyed, to send the noise away, but the pilot came even closer, forcing him to open his eyes.

At first the picture was blurry, ugly, and would in no way come together. Then, all of a sudden, his brain functioned, and the groan coming from his gut coincided with the Corfiot's, who managed to turn on his side, pressing on top of him.

"Mario, they're here..."

"Kick me, if you can, Spyros. I can't move. I'm completely numb."

Drawing strength from reserves they didn't suspect they had, the two men began their endeavour by pushing each other on the floor and, while the pilot gained altitude to give them time to pull themselves together and get ready, they managed to make their legs work through kicking, got to their feet, and continued jumping and hitting each other as if they were fighting.

"How are you doing, Spyros?"

Corfiot's faded eyes were now sparkling.

"Now? I can take on the world! I'll be like new in a minute."

"You see, wasn't I right to keep you till the end? Who else would take it like you have?"

The Corfiot stopped hitting himself, panting, and looked at Mario. "Let's get out of here first, and you'll have it later."

Mario took a look around them and felt the top part of his body getting needles and pins. "I wonder how we haven't hit the bottom yet. Get ready quickly; I'll signal him to come down."

"I'm OK. Call him, but you're going up first."

Mario suspended the gesture and looked at him in shock. "What are you babbling about, you Spyros? Leave the bullshit and get on with it, you're going up."

"I'm not going anywhere. Didn't you want me till the end? Well I'm staying till the end. At the end of the day, I'm a member of the crew and you aren't."

Mario tried in vain first to intimidate him and then to appeal to his better nature, as the Corfiot remained unyielding in his stubbornness, like a spoiled brat.

Spyros continued, "I've told you, I'm not going. If you want to, signal him for yourself. I'm not going up."

"You must have gone mad, Spyros. There's no other explanation. Do you want to flip for it?"

"Yes."

Mario searched quickly in his empty pockets. He looked around without success and pulled the beret off the Corfiot's head. "Which side are you calling?"

"The inside."

The greasy beret took off into the air, and the pilot thought it a signal and started descending. The hat was swept away by the wind and landed on the water, but they could both see who had won.

"Now that's more like it. I'll go up," Spyros conceded.

They were lucky and caught the strap on the first attempt. The Corfiot left more easily than they'd expected. Mario watched him going up for a while and then crawled toward the winch where he'd wedged the purse, stuffed it under his shirt, and fixed his gaze on the helicopter while his heartbeat was getting stronger and his incoherent thoughts transformed into loud utterances to keep him company.

His fingers worked fine when he longingly grabbed the wire, but it tautened suddenly, dragged him away, and he crashed with his back on the air duct. It was a heavy knock and scared him to death, but he didn't let go of the strap nor did he feel the pain.

Terrified at the thought that if something happened to him, there would be no one there to help him, he summoned up his entire concentration ability, found the perfect time to put on the strap and waved his hand to be hoisted.

His heart was pounding like crazy, as his body was flying blindly among the wires and the masts, but the person operating the winch had got the hang of it and was managing it well. Mario escaped the final dangerous obstacle of the antenna and sighed in relief. As his arms were up in the air, though, his clothes got loosened from his belt and the purse with the documents he'd stuck underneath hovered, ready to fall.

The abrupt, instinctive movement to catch it almost cost his life, as the strap slip down his left armpit and his eyes caught a glimpse of the raging sea bellow, making his blood run cold. With his heart in his mouth, he swung his body to the right and sucked his stomach in as much as possible to balance the purse on it. Careful not to move, he kept ascending without breathing, knowing fully well that on the first jolt he was doomed to fall.

The soldier suspended himself dangerously outside the aircraft, wrapped his free arm around Mario's waist, hugging the purse as well, and pulled him in instantly, dropping him next to the Corfiot, who was smiling tiredly.

Dusk had begun scattering its shadows as the helicopter turned around, en route to Cagliari, and the last image of the Salonica, half-lost in the spume, broke his heart.

"Mille grazie, amico."

The soldier had grown a moustache to look older, but his smile was still childlike.

"You should thank the captain. They wouldn't let him fly. He came back at his own risk."

Mario, moved, looked at the back of the man who had saved his life and cupped his hands.

"Grazie, capitano…"

The grey-haired captain's warm smile held something divine for Mario, and his look made words unnecessary. For a few moments, the two men let their eyes do the talking, then the captain nodded, content, and turned his attention to the storm.

The dark that had been enveloping quickly the narrow horizon and the droning noise lulled the exhausted Mario to sleep, but the smile remained on his face.

It had been raining hard in the nocturnal Cagliari when the helicopter touched ground next to the port authority. Mario had barely woken up from the Corfiot's push when the emergency services workers entered the aircraft.

Confused, he let them cover him with a blanket and carry him out, but refused to lie on a stretcher. He got cross with the blinding TV camera lights, stated that he only spoke Greek in order to avoid the questions, grabbed the brandy from the nurse's hand, and staggered after the Corfiot's stretcher, searching in vain for the captain so he could say goodbye.

"That's OK, Makis. I'm fine, let go of me now."

Sniffing and emotional, the engineer relaxed his embrace and wiped his eyes with his fingers. "I thought we wouldn't see each other again. When he headed off, I went mad. There was no reasoning with him. He said he was overloaded."

"He was right, but thankfully he came back. How have you been here?"

"Look at them. They're sleeping like babies. They don't give a sod..."

"Is Simos here, too? Shouldn't he be at the hospital?"

The engineer looked suspiciously toward the door and lowered his voice. "I asked him to be patient a while longer, and, besides, now that he's stepped on ground, he's feeling better already..."

"But why?"

"The plans have changed. There have been new developments."

"What do you mean?"

"Listen, Mario, for the moment, we're like any other shipwreck survivors, and they're taking good care of us. In the morning, though, when they start their preliminary inquiry, we'll get into trouble..."

"Have they not asked for your documents, or to speak to the captain?"

"They've asked for everything, but we played dumb. We communicated with gestures, and we pretended not to speak any languages and that our documents are at the bottom of the sea, and in the confusion, I sent the Italian to phone Signorino."

Mario got tense. "Had he heard the news?"

"He'd seen it on TV. The Italian said he sounded really down, but he arranged for us to sneak off on the first flight to Rome, and he'll be waiting for us there."

They slipped out like ghosts an hour before dawn, when the authority port building was dead quiet, and there was not a soul in sight. The two blokes waiting in their small fiats further down the road were cordial, but of few words, had their boots full of clothes, and had arranged everything.

They finished quickly at the airport, handed them the tickets, kissed them on the cheek, and left, without saying anything. The wind had abated, and in the first light the calm sea looked like it was mocking him. Mario pulled the little curtain down not to see it, looked absentmindedly at the flight attendant's legs, and his mind wandered off to Signorino.

CHAPTER 16

"It's impossible, Vincenzo. I'm tired. I've flipped out. I don't know how else to say it—my nerves..."

Signorino's gesture at the waiter to refresh their drinks was as classy as always, but he hadn't shaved for days, and the huge diamond was missing from his finger, along with his metallic voice.

"As much as you can, Mario. Even five voyages would be really important for me right now."

"Give me some time, Vincenzo. I won't make it. I need some time to pull myself together. I'm going mad, I'm telling you!"

The Italian downed his vodka and called the waiter again. "Unfortunately, Mario, we're running out of time. Many people have lost money, and if we don't move fast, we'll be in trouble."

"There's nothing we can do, Vincenzo. How can we move? The boat's at the bottom of the sea. We have to accept that."

"We'll try again, Mario. We still have the one that was delivered late. I've shipped it to Malta; you'll find it there."

"How about the cargo?"

Signorino looked at the mark from the ring on his finger and grimaced.

"I've bought a share in another squadra that works near us."

He nervously downed the fresh vodka and leaned forward. "I swear on our friendship, Mario, I know how you feel, but I desperately need a few voyages for cash inflow. Then you can rest, and I'll have time."

Mario knew this was a lost battle, but he couldn't help but throw down his last ace. "I don't even have an assistant—he left with the others for Greece..."

"Hire another one, Mario."

"Who?"

"Whoever you want. Take on the Maltese, you'll be flying with him to Valetta anyway."

"The Maltese? The young boy? After what he's been through? There's no way he would accept."

"Ask him."

They were flying over Sicily when he brought it up, and the youngster's answer astounded him.

"Aren't you scared of anything, you little bugger? It hasn't even been twenty-four hours since you were shipwrecked!"

The youngster's fuzzy cheeks blushed, but there was nothing heroic in his eyes. "I really need the job, Mario. My mother..."

His story was terribly sad, and Mario felt guilty for not being more sympathetic, as it had worked out conveniently for him. The younger had sailed through the shipwreck test, having been levelheaded and courageous when required, keen, and soft-spoken, an unexpected find for Mario, who had suddenly stumbled on his replacement, so he could leave the squadra smoothly.

"Listen, I'll put in a few more trips, and then I'll leave. If you do well, I'll recommend you for my position. Are you interested?"

The young Maltese's black eyes opened wide, his cheeks flushed, and despite his conscientious effort, he could not find the right words to express his gratitude. "Grazie, Mario."

"Don't mention it. It works for me as well."

Instructed by Signorino, the hotel manager and their man in Malta surpassed themselves in fulfilling and anticipating his every need. The days went by in a fashion that would have excited him in the past, but he didn't feel the same anymore. Mario, feeling like a lamb before slaughter, found it impossible to enjoy himself, while his nightmares became more frequent, and he systematically avoided visiting the port.

Giving his directions reluctantly from the hotel, their man and the young Maltese prepared the boat and arranged the rendezvous with the ship in the open water. The sea calmed, and Mario ran out of excuses for further delays.

In the afternoon of the fourth day, he decided to drag his feet to the port. He sulkily jumped on the boat, nodded at the youngster, and sailed off for the first voyage. Experienced sailors, the crew members were working fast, and the horizon looked free of threats. Mario got sucked in the flow of things, forgot his troubles, and before he even knew it, he'd completed two runs without the slightest problem.

He returned to sleep in Valetta at dawn, exhausted, but in a better mood. After so many days, his nightmares finally abated and allowed him time to rest. With the calm sea as his ally, which was still holding out mid-winter, as well as the young Maltese's invaluable assistance, the next three nights were adequately productive, and Mario was happily on his way back to spend his last night in Valetta. He was distracted with thoughts about Greece, and he didn't hear the youngster at first. The Maltese shouted again, pointing somewhere behind him in the dark, but when Mario turned to see, he was already late. The headlight blinded him, and the voice from the megaphone pierced his eardrums. Mario was stunned for a moment, but then he turned instinctively to the left to avoid the ramming and heard the first gun shot.

Dazzled by the light, he straightened the wheel, pushed the levers all the way forward, and started gaining distance, when he saw the flash from the second shot. The bullet ricocheted, whizzing past his head with a terrifying noise, sending a shudder through him while the sound of his own scream shocked him even more. "Oh, my God! That was close, brother!"

He leaned forward and became one with the dashboard, driving like crazy with constant zigzagging for a little while. When the headlight's strength faded and the burst of shots sounded amusing, the terror turned into fury. He showed his fist at the patrol boat and started swearing at them. He exhausted his thesaurus of swear words and turned to the Maltese. "Am I right or what, kiddo? The wankers thought they..."

He found it odd that he hadn't met the youngster's eyes at the same level. Then he looked down and laughed.

"Come on, get up. We're safe."

The youngster stayed still, and Mario was troubled for a moment. Then he felt so overwhelmed, he couldn't breathe. He pulled the levers back to stop the boat, jumped off his seat, and on his second step he slipped and landed next to his assistant.

Cursing his clumsiness, he rose to his knees. He tried to wipe his sticky hands on his trousers, but just then he realized what he'd slipped on, and his stomach churned. Frozen, unable to think, with his heart pounding, he stretched out his hand and turned him over.

The young man's wide-open, motionless eyes were looking at the stars, his mouth was half-open as if pondering, while the nightmarish black hole in his throat was still bleeding. Mario collapsed, his hands covered in blood, and puked there between them.

Proclaiming yet another beautiful day, the sun was releasing his first rays when Mario reached the port, tied the boat, and disappeared in the pier's phone booth. He had a short conversation, then went slowly up the hill, lit a cigarette, and waited. He was putting out his second when their man's car, with someone he didn't know at the wheel, stopped by the boat.

The two men got off, looked around them, and jumped on board. A minute later, they reappeared, carrying the young man's body, laid him in the back seat and sped off. Mario watched the car until it disappeared on the next turning and walked slowly to his hotel.

Half an hour later, cleaned up and in a different outfit, he went outside to the road again and hailed a taxi.

"To the airport, please!"

The taxi driver was young, slightly resembling his dead assistant, and felt like chatting.

"You are leaving? Will you be coming back soon?"

Mario had reached his decision long ago, so he replied with no hesitation: "Never!"

Easy comes, easy goes, then, my friend Nestor.

So, if I strove to put in words for you a handful of incidents from young Panagiotakis's odyssey, I've done it for your son, whom I cherish as my own.

And, so you should know, he's right when he says that the contraband has never stopped, and it is true that he would be getting handsomely paid. He is also justified in wanting to risk his youth, but he is gravely mistaken if he believes that our current technological advances have made this trade a child's play.

Remind him that grasses and helicopters have become obsolete, since satellites are not on the take and that, even though they will be following him everywhere, he will never see them.

As for the old, wrecked patrol boats that will only catch the backwash, remind him that they've already been replaced by powerful shuttles, which will be leading the dance in his nightmares.

Unfortunately, for aspiring fortune hunters like him, the balance has shifted and adventure doesn't taste half as sweet as it used to. Nevertheless, hardship is still wearing the same mantle and the danger of becoming a welcome meal for the trawl-net fish has never diminished.

Finally, if despite everything he still has his mind set on getting into trouble, I, my friend, have run out of arguments and give up; however, I do have one last wish for him:

Boca Lupo, my boy.

THE END